For my Adovey, Happy Birthday!

Parallel Worlds

Rachel Roy

Published by Rachel Roy Independent Publishing, 2023.

PARALLEL WORLDS

First edition. July 6, 2023.

ISBN: 979-8987431412

Written by Rachel Roy.

Table of Contents

Title Page 1

Parallel Worlds... 7

Chapter 1 - The Duel 8

Chapter 2 - The Message 21

Chapter 3 - The Meeting.. 27

Chapter 4 - Humanity and Houses................................ 36

Chapter 5 -The Plague 49

Chapter 6 - A Summons.. 69

Chapter 7 - Envoys 83

Chapter 8 - The Library... 93

Chapter 9 - Waiting.. 103

Chapter 10 - A little Pet 115

Chapter 11 - Reunited 124

Chapter 12 - Hide and Seek 136

Chapter 13 - Continue the Games............................... 149

Chapter 14 - Now What?!.. 156

Chapter 15 - Festivus Planning...167

Chapter 16 - Festivus 177

Prologue...191

Chapter 1 196

Table of Contents 199

PARALLEL WORLDS

By Rachel Roy

Chapter 1 - The Duel

Sitting in a staff meeting is almost never fun. All the memes created about it, prove the universal truth of the time waste of most meetings. *This coulda been an email...* The speaker kinda drones on and she strains to stay focussed. Crocheting or something to occupy her hands and some of her attention actually helps keep her thoughts from wandering and she can better focus on the speaker. Still, most staff meetings could easily be emails with interactive documents.

Staff meetings in the morning sometimes are made more sufferable by drinking coffee. Afternoon staff meetings with tepid water in a water bottle, light shining off white classroom walls and middle-school BO shadow wafting in the air, are not so pleasant. Seventeen adults circled around tables in a rough U shape, with the principal speaking to them from the front.

To be fair, he kept it as lively as possible, and was good at gauging the attention and emotion of his audience. Suddenly, a muffled commotion in the hallway catches her ear. Turning her head quickly catches the attention of the Humanities and Math teachers across the U. As the muffled noises come closer it becomes apparent that the scuffling is a group of people coming down the hall towards their room. Her senses tingle, the air is suddenly charged as if before a lightning strike. As the first face passes the door window, she mutters "Fuck me!"

Several faces turn quickly to her and then follow her gaze to the window as she stands up. Her chair scraping against the floor.

"Sorry," she mumbles to the principal as she rushes towards the door. "Fuck me running, not here-" As the second door bangs open and the scuffle of energetic men start pouring in, as she tries to motion them back out of the room. As soon as they see her, they stop talking but they continue pushing into the room. "Ah, no, Lass. Here is where we be." The tall, broad shouldered, military attitude of a man stands square in front of her, clearly empathetic but clearly not retreating.

"Shit."

"Indeed." The side of his mouth briefly turned up in commiseration.

Turning over her shoulder, she said to the meeting at large, "Apparently this is going to interrupt you for a moment. Sorry. Can one of you bring my computer and stuff to my desk, when you're done?" Then striding forward, she balanced on one leg, lifting her other foot to rest on her knee and began untying her shoe. "Begin Captain," she said to the only man of the group to have spoken. Nodding once, with a look of approval, he began to speak in another language.

His voice was gruff but strong, and clearly spoke the words of a ritual. As he spoke, men behind him formed into a semblance of order, not standing at attention, but standing formally. One man stepped forward with an armload of leather belts, wraps, sheaths, and knives. With the weapons offered, he stood ready, but waiting.

She pulled out her ponytail hair-tie with her right hand, and shook her hair loose, then her fingers deftly braided her hair. At the same time she snapped her fingers towards one of the

other men, catching his eye, and nodding towards the staff
group behind her. Nodding quickly the man stepped closer to
the teachers in the meeting. Clearing his throat softly to catch
their attention he said, "Afternoon, I um, I imagine you are a
bit surprised with us showing up here. Begging your pardon
for the interruption." He smiled disarmingly and continued,
"She's pretty amazing you know. But as she just pointed out,
you probably would like some clarification. Does any of you
understand what they are saying, by chance?" He paused,
looking across the group.

"Come again now, speak what?" asked the Humanities teacher.

"Right," nodded the young man. "And none of you know
Aegnyan, right?"

Seeing no one looking confident with an answer he continued
on. "Ok then. Quick background. This woman you know as
Arichel is probably a dedicated, hard working woman here in
your world. She is also the Queen of Aegnya in my world. Yes,
let me just pause while that sinks in. I'm guessing that you
didn't know that there were parallel worlds. There are. Let's
just agree to move forward as if you believe that statement to
be true. Queen Arichel has just been challenged to a Blood
Duel. This is an ancient rite, so ancient we know it predates our
written history. While some of the motions may have changed
some, much of it is ritualized and must be completed just so.
It is legally binding though, used about only once in a lifetime.
Last time it was called upon was during her grandmother's
reign. Now that the ceremony has begun, it may be paused for
up to one passing day and one passing night, but it may not be
stopped. The results are binding. This is what you might call a
'duel for the right to rule' ."

"A duel?"

"Yes."

"To the death?!?"

"Perhaps." "What?!?"

"Right now Queen Arichel is being reminded of our people's history. Truthfully, it may be a chance for the fighter to gather their thoughts and focus for there has never been a sitting queen who does not know every historical event of her people. She is also being blessed. And, because she was the one surprised, umm, *invited,* to the Blood Duel she is also physically preparing for her battle."

While the young man was explaining, and while the gruff man was ritually speaking, Arichel hadn't stopped moving. After removing her shoes, then braiding her hair, she grabbed the topmost knife from the armload displayed to her. Surprising the staff members, she quickly sliced open her jeans at the inside of her knees and the ankle cuff. Then she slipped the knife back into a sheath and strapped it inside her pant leg against her calf. She did the same to the other leg. Another soldier stepped forward with leather boots, she slipped on the tall boots, lacing them up to just even with where the handle of the knives were hidden. Surprisingly, the boots had three inch heels. She then tucked several more knives into the cuffs of the boots, and two tiny blades hidden under the laces by her toes.

"You can see her preparing for the physical fight right now. Slicing the material at her knees allows for greater mobility. When she walks out of this room, she will be carrying a variety of blades, ready for use. She is the most dangerous person you know." The soldier did his best to offer an explanation, while not overwhelming his students.

Just then, a new group of men burst through the door. Catching the eye of the man in the lead, with a quick shake of her head, Arichel ritualistically spoke and the captain continued speaking as if there had been no interruption. Words were swallowed on the lips of the man entering and he motioned his men to be silent. They respectfully and quietly shuffled into the room.

"That's MacKeritt." a shocked, hushed exclamation. The newcomer glanced over, acknowledging the speaker with a tip of an imaginary hat.

"Who?" asked another teacher.

"The leader of the IRA."

"Oh!"

As the ritual continued, Arichel again shocking the teachers, ripped her shirt up over her head and clearly showed a back covered in long scars and vibrant tattoos. Quickly, she strapped knives with various ties of leather about her arms, and ribs. A loose shirt akin to a tank top slipped over her weapons. Then two more large knives were strapped to either side of her waist. The Captain paused, and Arichel renewed eye contact to MaKeritt.

The young soldier explained to the teachers, "Now is a moment in the ritual that others are invited to speak and add their knowledge to hers." As MacKeritt spoke in the same language as the ritual, the soldier translated. "He says, that as always his people support Queen Arichel, which is a surprise to most of us, I expect. Although she doesn't seem a bit surprised, nor does Captain." The soldier seemed to be musing aloud as much as explaining. He implores her to remember her strengths and to ...draw her energy from the earth and the sky. He says the

Mother will always nurture her." He shook his head. "That is not what I expected at all."

Arichel inclined her head at MacKeritt and spoke back, clearly a formal thank you. She returned her attention to the Captain. She knelt, and he placed his hands on her shoulders, then to her head, while speaking some more formal words. Then, he took her hand and raised her to her feet. Immediately, all the men from both groups, though the second group was just a tad slower as if they hadn't known, dropped to a knee and bowed their heads.

She spoke a single word, looking at those kneeling. Then the mood changed. All the men stood up, and most relaxed their stance. Some still seemed tense. Glancing back at the teachers and principals, she tilted her head, raised an eyebrow and said, 'Let's get this party started, shall we?" Slinging a long scabbard onto her back, she stepped back from the group and withdrew a long, two handed broadsword. She swung it around and found the balance. "It'll do." She resheathed it. "You needn't come, but you are welcome to watch if you want." She strode out through the door to the hall. Her co-workers, glanced at each other in confusion, then pushed back chairs to follow. "What the *hell* is happening here?" whispered the Special Education teacher. None of his coworkers knew how to answer. Passing through the hall, someone asked her, "How are you not nervous?"

"What will be, will be." After a half moment's pause she continued, "He's well trained, but so am I. Don't forget his dancing teacher learned from me." After a slightly longer pause, she stated, "Today is a good day to die. But, I do not intend to die this day."

Another commotion behind them caused Arichel to spin back around. Seeing the young boy running towards them, weighed down by a long bundle with some sort of silver dog's head at one end, she quickly halted. She pulled off the scabbard and held it off to the side without looking. One of the soldiers took the sheathed sword. The boy ran directly to her, with ragged breath. She knelt down to look directly in his eyes. "Elden, thank you." Then she pulled back the cloth, revealing not a dog's head but a gorgeous wolf pommeled broadsword. She swung that scabbard onto her back and spun back around, not even bothering to test the blade, she simply reached up and tugged slightly to be sure the blade slid freely.

Just before they exited the building Adovey grabbed her lightly on the arm. Immediately, she turned to him and gave him a tight smile. Leaning forward she said "I love you," and kissed him. Pulling back, she was about to turn and go, when he pulled her back.

Growling, "Fuck *that*." he pulled her in for a deep kiss, tongue thrusting against her mouth, and lips hungrily devouring hers. She matched every bit of his ardor, pressing her body, and all the hilts, against him. None of the men seemed at all surprised though a few seemed a bit envious. Their kiss ended and he looked deep in her eyes.

"Yeah," she said, nodding.

"I love you, too," he said.

Then, she turned and pushed open the doors. Most of the group came to an abrupt halt as they exited the building and saw another group of soldiers standing. Arichel however strode forward, across the dirt parking spots, to the little hill. "It's mostly flat up here."

A tall and surprising slender soldier from the middle of the group standing outside nodded approval and followed her up. "Agreed."

The two squared off, both Arichel and Bryongan Le Bryon sideways to the sun, so neither had an advantage starting out. "Blessed met," he said to her.

"Blessed be," She raised her hands up, palms out and he placed his hands against hers. Then, they each stepped back and rubbed their hands together.

The young soldier again cleared his throat, and then began speaking. "This is a ritual challenge as I said, and there are certain steps they do now to follow that ritual. They share the blessings as they hope their people to be blessed. They press palms together and then rub their hands together so no one has an advantage of a stickiness or oiliness hindering or helping. They have now stepped back to have room to draw the weapons of their choice to begin.

"You might notice," the young soldier continued, "that they each have several weapons on their person that can be seen. More than likely they also have several weapons that cannot be seen. Now, they draw when ready and fight until a victor is mutually agreed upon by the two of them."

"Or, when one of them is dead," inserted a gruff voice from the opposing soldiers.

"Aye, when one dies or they agree. That is the end of combat and the decision that binds."

"Might as well get comfortable, boys." The captain included the soldiers of both groups. "Likely we'll be here a while. Kian, how is that brother of yours doing?" The soldiers intermingled, obviously knowing each other well, and not seeming at odds with each other. They stood or sat, a bit spread out, but more or less together along one side so as not to be an obstruction. Their attention was rapt on the two in the center, who had slowly begun to circle each other.

Arichel was mentally checking herself and her body, what muscles might need to stretch, if any bindings were a touch too tight, and all the while watching exactly how Bryongan stepped. Watching and analyzing, not even really thinking about it, but absorbing the information. Almost as one, they drew their long swords. Bryongan withdrew a broadsword from a scabbard at his side. It seemed to fit well in one hand, but better in two. The light seemed to be absorbed into the metal neither reflecting or refracting, not glowing, not swallowing, but just absorbing the light. Arichel pulled hers from the scabbard on her back. At the same time, she shrugged, letting the scabbard fall from her shoulder, letting it drop down, and then stepping out and kicking it out of the way. As she pulled the sword overhead and then held it in both hands. She let the tip lower near the ground in front of her, relaxing her shoulders. Slowly, she circled Bryongan as he circled back. The light glittered off the blade and made the wolf's eyes glitter bright green.

"What type of sword is that?" breathed one of the men.

"That sword is Wolfsbane," answered the young soldier.

"Damascus steel and freely given to our queen by King Daviraf Dafang of the Lumos people," stated the captain with pride.

"The Lumo-"

"Wolfsbane?!?"

"No way!"

"But isn't th-"

The young soldier spoke again to the group of teachers. "Wolfsbane is an herb said to repel werewolves, if you believe in such."

"Ahh. Lumos as in moon," commented the principal, the first he had spoken since his meeting had been so thoroughly interrupted.

"Yes, Lumos, *of the moon*, has led to many, umm...speculations about the people who live there. The symbolism was completely implied when King Dafang gave the blade willingly to Queen Arichel when they promised their undying alliance and peace between our kingdoms. It is said that hundreds of years ago it was only that blade that was able to save the world from the maddest, fiercest werewolf known to exist. The eyes of the wolf are emerald, which is quite a soft gem and almost never used upon a weapon. The metal is Erin Damascus steel. It is incredibly rare, for the process to forge it is intricate, but it produces the strongest steel known." The young soldier was very good at sharing the information without any hint of a lecturing tone, but more like a conversation.

"It is also quite heavy, but perfectly balanced," stated the captain. "Those two are among the best blademasters I know, and their swords are fitting their status. A good lad there, young Elden, who was able to bring the blade to our queen." The young boy reddened at the praise, and ducked his head.

The battle scene stretches over hours, the setting sun lighting the blades on fire; the sky turned to dusk when shadows jump from nothing at all and movement slides into missing space. He draws first blood on her, a scratch, and he comments that she did that on purpose. She flashes a smile, but says nothing. They both have started breathing hard, but neither is out of breath.

They both move fluidly and almost constantly like a dance, with no wasted motions just like water moving in a stream, or a current in a lake.

Neither dancer seems to move many steps at a time and yet they have trampled down the grass in a large area. Eventually, a few hours after dusk, as it became dark and the temperature dropped, the soldiers start a fire in the middle of the dirt lot, down the small slope from the duel. The light is far enough away to not blind either swordmaster, but enough to cause dancing shadows leaping less gracefully all around them and twinkling off their own blades.

"Please pause and defend, while I state a question." The captain had moved closer and called out clearly to the duelists.They both stepped back an equal distance, but neither looked to the captain.

"Thank you. I ask you to pause, wondering whether you would like lanterns or torches put around this area to shed more light for you?" Again the captain spoke loud and clear.

Just as clearly, Arichel responded quickly before the other could speak. "I care not. My challenger may choose."

"Shit!" grumbled Bryongan, "Now either way you can claim an outcome was because of my choice regarding the lights." Arichel grinned in response. "Nay then, the moon will rise soon and give us light."

"Good then. Please mark my count to five and continue. One. Two. Three. Four. Five. Continue." The captain stepped back as he counted steadily and evenly, and on the final word, Arichel and Bryongan nodded to each other and stepped forward again.

They continued to dance, first meeting blades high then low, turning left and stepping right, moving left then right and right again, always flowing but with bone jarring hits of blade against blade. Suddenly dropping to one knee and blocking her head with the longsword in her left arm, a knife seemed to materialize in her right hand and she sliced through the arm straps on his left wrist. She rolled back and was on her toes, knees bent, in a moment. While her facial expression never changed, she had lost feeling for a moment and now suffered severe pins and needles in her left hand and forearm from absorbing the blow he had delivered. Worth it to her though, for putting him at a disadvantage for ruining his wrist brace on his dominant hand. Strength would come back to her arm, and if she was lucky, he wouldn't assume the truth and press her on that side. He was an experienced fighter though and did try to press the arm that he knew he had potentially stressed. She yielded steadily until they had made a full circle.

As expected, the moon rose over the mountains, shedding plenty of light. In that light it became apparent that Bryongan was bleeding from multiple cuts and scratches.His clothes were slashed with cuts criss-crossing his skin. He looked a bit like a mouse that had been toyed with by a cat. There was no great amount of bloodloss, but each wound was also a wound to his ego. By comparison, Arichel had only bled from the first slice, and her clothes were only tattered where she had sliced them at the knee. Arichel was fighting this battle both mentally and physically. Bryongan's thrusts from the left had less power now as his arm had lost that brace. She was able to keep turning him and forcing him to use that tired arm. Now he was battling himself as much as he was fighting her.

Suddenly, the captain stood more alert. "What do you see?" queried one of the other soldiers. Quickly they all stood alert, their full attention on the duelists. The boy leaned closer to the adults, "I don't see anything?"

"Look," the captain leaned down to the boy, "see their lips moving.They're discussing something. They're still dancing, but their blades be more quiet now." Indeed, steel hadn't been hitting steel as often.

Suddenly, Bryongan dropped to his knees and handed Arichel his sword, pommel extended. She snatched it and swung it at his neck. The lad gasped, but no one moved. They knew it was her choice how she would end the duel. She turned the blade at the last minute, nicking the tops of both ears as she brought the sword up and over his head to rest on first one shoulder and then the other. Then, holding his sword in her left hand, she sheathed her sword, then reached down and pulled up Bryongan with her right hand. She extended his sword to him. He nodded and sheathed his sword. Together they walked to the soldiers and spectators on the edge of the field. Two soldiers handed each of them a glass bottle of water and then a silver canteen. Arichel and Bryongan clinked their bottles together and drank deep, swallowing all the water without taking a breath. Then, they each dropped to the ground, as if collapsing from exhaustion. They drank deep from their canteens and lay back, staring up into the night sky hidden by the light from the fires.

Chapter 2 - The Message

The rain steadily dripped and rolled down the windows. The room had a slight dampness from a day of rain, but the wood heat mostly kept the damp at bay.

"It doesn't work you know - trying to live two lives. I mean we have plenty of time, but there's always complications."

He was right, she knew. She rubbed her temples as the headache thrummed, not that far away from terrible.

"Yeah. I know." She pushed back her chair and stood up. "I need coffee. Want some?" As she stood there, she shook out her ponytail to loosen the pull against her temples. Her very straight blown hair fell down about three quarters the length of her back. She rolled her shoulders and stretched her neck side to side. Her blue eyes pierced him to his soul and he knew better than to comment or ask about the headache. There wasn't any fixing it.

"Yeah, a cuppa would be good." He nodded, and turned to peer through the slightly foggy window out to the rain. "It's really raining hard now. Hopefully, they travel safe." Turning his head towards her, a smile in his voice, "None of that sweet grog now, just plain tea."

Laughing she said, "Just plain? So tea and cream?"

"Right."

She spun on her heel and went out and down to the kitchen. Along the way, numerous people met her and talked to her about their urgent ideas as they walked. She poured out several cups of coffee to those speaking with her and made a fresh pot. An inconvenience to the piles of paperwork on her desk, but a welcome distraction too. She heated the water and steeped some dark tea. Finally, enough coffee was in the glass carafe to fill her mug, and she prepared them both with a slurp of fresh cream and a bit of sugar. Catching the eye of one of the kitchen ladies she got a smile and a nod.

More coffee and tea would be sent up in a bit without the need for ringing for it. Walking back to her library had three more people chatting with her.

Gratefully, she quickly closed the door, almost on the nose, of the minister of interior. "Of course. We'll set a time to talk about it later." She dropped down into a big chair at the round table instead of at her desk, and blew a strand of hair from her face. She closed her eyes and sipped some coffee. Letting it fuel her body and mind. Only a minute's respite, then she looked up to Adovey and grabbed a pen and paper. "Ok, let's prioritize. What needs to be done now and what needs to be done soon?" Adovey sat down heavily in the chair opposite. "Mmhmm. Ok, let's think. We have the..."

Together they created a plan together, not always agreeing on the most important needs, but at least agreeing on the order to generally prioritize. The Captain had direction for how the troops could support the people and realistically be training at the same time. She might have a peaceful land, but every land had people who seek more power than they have, or seek land and property that isn't theirs.

***

"M'lady, m'lady come quick!" On the heels of the young page running in, came the official herald with more decorum, if less grace.

"Your highness," he said slightly out of breath, "please excuse our interruption." He glared at the young page who turned bright red and stared at the floor. "It is imperative that we have a moment of your time. Startling news has come from the north, and I think you will want to read this yourself." Long practice at his job made him very good at deciding levels of priority. Knowing her so well, let him convey all sorts of news without actually sharing anything to whatever other ears might be near her at any given time.

"Thank you, Mercury, please sit. Everyone else, why don't we recess for a bit?" Phrased as a question, but not actually asked, Arichel dismissed everyone else in the room. Catching Adovey's eye, she made sure he knew to stay. "Lad," she spoke softly to the young page, "you may stay or go, it is up to you." Still a bit pink faced, he glanced up at the messenger and seeing his smiling nod, he gratefully backed out of the room.

"Holy Shit!" breathed Arichel as she slipped to the floor. In some places, a queen sitting on the floor might be an indication of abject despondency or failure. Anyone who knew Arichel was used to her randomly sitting on the floor or the ground, or perching on furniture, just as often as she walked around barefoot. And she did that almost all the time, even in the snow!

She held out the message and Adovey read it. "Well, fuck," he said. "We need our Inner Circle, now."

"Yeah, I called them."

"That mindspeak thing is awfully handy, yknow?" He gave a sad grin.

"Uhhuh," she agreed. "Captain is at the training grounds, but he'll be here shortly, Lath will be here this afternoon, probably because of that little stir up the other day"

Adovey snorted at her describing a Death Duel as a "little stir up".

On the heels of her words the door burst open and Kribell came in. Her petite size, completely dwarfed by her obvious temper. Her hair swung around her face as she dropped to the arm of the chair next to Arichel. "Who the *actual hell* is attacking children?!"

Arichel handed her the note and Adovey handed her a glass of red wine. She completely ignored the glass as she read the note and then grabbed and gulped half the glass at once. Adovey steadied the glass and refilled it for her. He then handed a glass to Arichel, as well. She nodded her thanks and took a soothing drink.

"Well, holy hell," said Kribell

Through the door strode both Jarrandon and Riveya. "I will not tolerate our children being harmed." The dark aloof woman brooked no tone for argument. However she met none. Adovey handed a glass of wine so dark it was a blackish purple to Jarrandon and nodded to Riveya.

Jarrandon smiled disarmingly as he handed it off to Riveya. He was one of the few willing to cross her tongue and she knew it. "It's why we are here at a moment's notice, Riv. None of us want anything to happen to the children." Adovey handed a glass of beer to Jarrandon, while wiping some foam off his own lip.

"Lath will be here this afternoon, but we're not to wait," said Arichel.

"So we know that border towns are reporting that they are missing children. At first it was just one or two here and there and people thought that they were runaways. Unusual but not unheard of. Except they are now realizing that the numbers are higher than usual. Today, there was a business convention and suddenly it was talked about. As soon as they realized, it was reported to us that this is happening

The children are disappearing without any obvious pattern. The border towns are the ones who have reported in-"

"Which borders?" asked Jarrandan.

"Our borders with Nordreich and Attalia." answered Arichel.

"Eierin is having a similar problem." stated Jarrandon. I'll see if anyone else is. He stood up and hurried out to reach out to his intelligence network.

"So first," mused Adovey while pouring himself another beer and then shaking some salt in, watching it foam up, "we need to know whether the children are leaving by choice or not."

"I think we need to find the children first," rebuffed Riveya. "I don't know that we care why they left."

"Oh but we do. We do care very much, Riv." said Kribell. "Perhaps they are enticed, but perhaps they are kidnapped. Is this some wild adventure story they think has come to life, or is this an act of war?"

The huge world map on the wall was studied, and a large map of their kingdom and the surrounding kingdoms was laid out on the conference table. Tallies of missing children were marked on the table map and to their chagrin, it soon became apparent that there were many, many missing children. Higher numbers were in the border towns, but children were missing from all the territories of all the countries. The country of Prushka didn't really want to share any details, but they grudgingly admitted to some missing children, especially along the border.

After sifting through information and new reports all night, it was decided that an international meeting must be called. Adovey was tasked with the job of picking the time and settling an agreed upon location for all the heads of state and their courts to meet. The sooner the better. "If anyone can find an agreeable location in less than a month, it would be your golden tongue, Adovey. We need to meet *now*!" Disturbed and worried, they went to bed late with heavy hearts. Who would be stealing the children? And why?

Chapter 3 - The Meeting

Three days later, the Inner Circle of the Royal Court of Aegnya, gathered at the conference table. They were an interesting mix of personalities from the svelte Riv to the grizzly Captain. Part of what made the Inner Circle so intelligent was the diverse nature and knowledge of its members. The unbreakable bond that held the Inner Circle together was their absolute trust in each other. Their diverse backgrounds often made their opinions clash, but under it all they had mad respect for each other. Through the years they had each saved the other's lives countless number of times. That tends to seal bonds between friends. The humor needed to deal with each other's ridiculous opinions and absolute embarrassments, helped too. Regardless of their diverse opinions and priorities, protecting children was at the top.

"I'm impressed, Adovey, that you were able to get everyone to agree on a location so quickly. Actually, I'm impressed they agreed on a location at all."

"Well," laughed Adovey quietly, "if you imply that everyone else has already agreed to this location or someplace that no one wants to go, you get an agreed upon location pretty quickly."

"What a negotiator," agreed Lath laughing.

"It's probably a bad idea to start drinking before we go, right?" asked Arichel, only half joking.

"Probably you should wait," chuckled Adovey. "I'll make sure you get a glass there."

Arichel grimaced but nodded her agreement. "All right then, shall we?" She stood up and threw her gray cloak over her shoulders. "Let's go."

***

Voices traveled down the hall to them as the Inner Circle bunched up inside the door. Immediately, there were pages that offered to take their coats.

Arichel warmly smiled her thanks at a frecklefaced boy as he slipped her coat over his arm. She held out her hand as if to tip him, just as an adult butler greeting fine guests would receive. After a half second's pause he held out his hand to accept her tip and then smiled widely when he saw the maple drop in his palm. She winked at him then, knowing the candy delicacy was hard to get elsewhere than her kingdom. Eyes wide he popped the candy in his mouth and then bowed so low her coat dragged on the floor.

Meanwhile, the voices had stopped as King Tinkerrtin peered out the door. "Aha, I did feel the draft. See, I'm not imagining it." Waving his hand impatiently the king smiled and beckoned them into the room he was at. As Lath passed King Tinkerrtin murmured. "Thank the gods you're here, I'm about to kill this pompous windbag!"

Lath choked on a laugh as he kept walking in and so Jarrendon walked straight to the bar and poured two glasses of wine: one for poor Lath and one for Arichel who blew him a kiss as he walked towards her.

"Yes, yes. You must be parched from your journey!" exclaimed King Tinkerrtin brightly. "Let's all have a drink toasting everyone's safe travels! And, my sanity." The last bit was said much quieter and Arichel snorted a laugh as she turned away from Sir Windham quickly, so the 'pompous windbag' wouldn't see her laugh.

"Sir Windham, I'm glad to see you were able to make it," said Queen Arichel smoothly a moment later with a warm smile. "We do want everyone's views on the problem at hand."

"Ahem. Yes well. Complete waste of time if you ask me." Sir Windham's eyebrows jumped ferociously up and down his forehead much faster than his words stumbled out of his mouth. "Ahem. Foolish waste of time, these children running off in the woods pretending to adventure. Ahem, silly waste of a royal meeting."

"Oh, so have you noticed the disappearance of children, too, Sir Windham?" asked Jarrandon. "I thought your reply to my query was that there were no missing children in your province." Jarrandon spoke jovially but Kribell noticed the fingers gripping the wine glass were white with a bright dot of red at each nail as he squeezed so hard he might shatter the glass. Swiftly, she reached forward and clasped the glass. "Oh, please, let me taste a sip of this and see if it tastes as good as it smells."

Jarrandon tossed her a smile and turned back to Sir Windham. "I'm sorry, I'm just a bit confused."

"Ahem. Well no, well yes, but no, nothing unusual." Sir Windham stumbled through his answer. "Yes, a very few children are unaccounted for, but really, ahem, it's quite normal for some children to run off and seek an adventure chasing dragons or some such foolishness."

"Uhhuh, and how many foolish adventurers are "unaccounted" for?" asked Jarrandon.

Both Queen Arichel and King Tinkerrtin were listening carefully to the exchange. They didn't even have to pretend at small talk while they did so.

"Ahem, well not many, ahem about thirty one, I, ahem, I suppose."

"THIRTY ONE?" roared Jarrandon. "Thirty one children are UNACCOUNTED for? Your total island's population is only 430!" You don't think THIRTY ONE is a trifle LOT of children? On a miserable

ISLAND to boot?"

Kri handed him back his glass of wine and Jarrandon swallowed it in one gulp. Then, he stood there breathing heavily as he gathered his emotions back in check.

"Ahem. Well. No need to shout at me."

The doors swung in then as Queen Eleynia swayed in. Jarrandon spun on his heel to glare out the window and accepted another glass of whiskey from Adovey without a word. He quickly snapped it back, and took a deep breath through his nose. Adovey then switched out the empty shot glass for another glass of the red wine. Jarrandon grunted his thanks and Adovey chuckled. "Infuriating man."

"Uhhuh," grunted Jarrandon. "If we didn't need his information, I might just pluck every hair from his body just to see if he notices those missing."

Adovey tipped his head back and laughed, truly enjoying the image.

Meanwhile, King Tinkerrtin had sailed over to meet Queen Eleynia and King Daviraf as they swished through the door. "Please come in!"

Slowly, everyone came in and chatted about any number of subjects, always with the missing children being talked about. Soon, everyone grew tired of Sir Pompous Windbag pushing off the obvious issue. But not quite everyone... The cocktail hour waned and still the Prushka royal court had not arrived. Some other countries had sent just ambassadors and most sent the full royal courts, but everyone had sent someone except Prushka. Adovey as the organizer went to speak with Tinkerrtin, the host. After a quick, hushed conversation, Tinkerrtin addressed the group.

"Alright everyone, we seem to have all arrived except for the Prushka delegation. I suggest that you all retire to your rooms for a bit and freshen up before our dinner. I will contact Prushka to see what the delay is. Dinner will be at 5, so that we may begin the purpose of this visit directly after."

The crowd nodded in agreement, and then Tinkerrtin finished in a sad tone, "We'll sup first, for I fear our discussions will run late."

***

The day that brings the bright moon, and lightning strikes twice from the sky, It shall be that day the red child is born, the fall shall bring forth a new fury.

The two halves carry destruction of the world with death of millions, When the moment comes before the last one dies, a challenge shall usher in. Wolves howl together, a promise broken, fury arrives in the white chariot of death, Once the last one dies, shall rise the true, and end all of history. "Yeah no, it does mention children," agreed Lath. "But it also mentions lightning and wolves, and like every other damned prophesy it doesn't say a damned thing."

"Why darling," laughed Eleynia, "it says there will be two lightening strikes from the sky. I mean at least we don't have to worry about lightning from the sea."

Jarrandon snorted and swirled the amber whiskey in his glass.

"Well, I would see, ahh, I see that you would try to steer this prophecy away from the real target." said Sir Windham.

"And what, do you think, the *real* target is?" purred Eleynia.

Arichel sent a mental hug at both Eleynia and Daviraf; he gave her a half smile back. Arichel had an idea where the pompous windbag was headed.

"Well, ahh, clearly, I mean it couldn't be more clear," started Sir Windham.

"Spit it out, man," growled Lath.

"Well, it ah, *clearly* states the wolves are at fault. That has to be Lumos, of course."

"You are nothing," said Adovey quickly, "if not predictable. About the only thing we can be sure of is that the werewolves are not to blame, no prophecy has ever been so clear as to state information directly."

Lath rolled his eyes and nodded to Arichel, who's frown lessened a little.

"I suppose, your idea has some, *little*, level of validity," said Lath quietly. "But I think we might want to keep looking at it." He slung back the last of his whiskey and Tinkerrtin immediately slid another glass down the table to him. Lath nodded his thanks.

"I think it would be handy to know how we're to know when the last ones are about to die," mused Eleynia. "That seems fairly climatic."

"And the white chariot of death," added Jarrandon.

"Doesn't death usually ride a black horse, why is he switching to white?"

"I thought Death was a woman?" asked Kribell with a sly smile. "Maybe she wants a new style."

"Hey, Sir Windham," poked Jarrandon, "where did you get your white chariot?"

"Ooh-hoo!" laughed Lath at the overwhelming blusterings coming from Sir Windham then.

"Maybe we should move off the prophecy for now," suggested King Bryongan, ever the diplomat. "It bears looking into, whether anyone else has prophecies that seem similar, but this is what our priests and priestesses are to solve, not us."

Several pensive looks were aimed at Bryongan. Previously he had been the one to smooth things over any time the ribbing was too much, or tempers flared. So why then, had he challenged Arichel to a duel. Arichel had dictated that no one should ask him or her about details like that. But dictates did nothing to end curiosity or even gossip. Conversations were sometimes tense for a few minutes just after falling back on the patterns of decades when a sudden flash of the duel came to mind. Was Bryongan the one to smooth things over or the one to stir up tension?

Adovey seemed to snap back into the conversation after being caught in his own thoughts for a moment. "Wait, what did you say about falcons?"

"I said," repeated McLaughlin with a twinkle in his eye, "that we have had an influx of falcons over the past few months. While falcons aren't afraid of the sea, and often nest along the sea coast, we don't usually have these numbers. Where last year we might have had ten mated pairs, we now have seventy."

Jarrandon whistled and Riv looked curious.

McLaughlin continued, "These numbers of predators have decimated the small prey along that area and now there is much fighting between the falcons themselves. It sounds like murdering chaos there each day with their whistles and screams."

"Well that's different," said Riv. "What the hell brought the birds out?" "And has anyone noticed they're missing elsewhere?" asked Lath.

"This can't be related to the missing children, but what *the hell* does it mean?" grumbled Tinkerton. He stood suddenly and began pacing. The others pushed back their chairs and stretched out arms or legs. It was as if their thoughts had started circling tightly and they needed to physically stretch themselves out, to break their thoughts out.

"We're missing something, not to state the obvious," growled Adovey.

"Yeah," assented the others, even Sir Windham.

McLaughlin stated, "You're right. We need more information. It's one thing to say we'll have the clerics work on the prophecy, but we need to collect more."

Jarrandon had been jotting notes. He looked up, "We need to know more about the missing children. We know that there doesn't seem to be a pattern of where they are from, except that the further inland the safer they seem to be. We need to know if they are similar in age, their families' occupations, ...anything."

Daviraf nodded. "That's what we do next. We collect as much information as we can, as quickly as possible. Jarrandon, will you be point on this? We all send information to you and you relay it out?" Davarif gave a wolfish smile, "I seem to recall you are excellent at gathering information."

Jarrandon nodded, while scribbling a note and missed the pointed smile. "Yes, send it to me. I'll annotate it and share the information daily. Or, more often if warranted."

Sir Windham popped up, "How do we know that everyone will honestly search?"

"Why? Is there someone in our midst who isn't trustworthy?" Adovey turned to him.

Sir Windham shrank back, "I, ahh, that is, I ah, no. I guess not, but we must consider it, mustn't we?"

"He's not wrong," Jarrandon agreed grudgingly. "But by gathering all the information together we should start to see patterns aligning, and the outliers." The others nodded. "I think we need to see if there are any other prophecies that might relate. I know," he held up a hand to forestall the arguments, "I know prophecies are, umm, *unreliable*. And there are

hundreds if not thousands. But just maybe there is a clue there."

Chapter 4 - Humanity and Houses

"I don't want to go back right now!" she raged.

"I know, but you have to." His voice was purposely calm and empathetic. He knew exactly how she felt. "We both have to."

"But the children are missing *here*!" Arichel continued to rage. "*Not* there."

"Yes," agreed Adovey, just as angry and just as frustrated as she was. "and the bargain must be upheld."

"Damnit."

He quirked an eyebrow, testing her ire.

"I know we need to go back to meet the terms of the bargain. But gods damn it. I don't want to." Arichel had moved onto the pacing anger now. The burning emotion, but available to plan again.

"Ok, so how do we go back and continue working on this? You can continue sifting through the histories, the forgotten lore to see if anything relates to the prophecy." Adovey was making the best suggestions he could and she knew it. But they still weren't good suggestions.

"But I want to be doing something! Finding them. Finding who took them and find out why."

"Obviously." Adovey grunted.

"Yeah, I know." Arichel smiled at him. He wasn't what she was mad at. She was angry that her heritage literally made her part of the glue that held the universe together. She, and others from her ancient family, had to travel between the two parallel worlds frequently. It was like their movements stitched the worlds or the planes together. It was easier to think of it as planes, when one considered how they were held or stitched together. But, clearly they were separate worlds as soon as you looked into the sky. Nothing about the suns, moons, and stars were the same.

"Ok, realistically I can do almost as much there in terms of email and reading. Jarandon can hold it together here putting things onto the map. It's no different than any other crisis."

"Right," agreed Adovey. "Kri, Lath, and Riv are all traveling first thing in the morning to research more on the coast. So no one will be here tomorrow anyway."

"Yeah." Arichel quit pacing and went towards Adovey. He enveloped her in his arms, her head against his shoulder. She loved how his strong arms could just surround her. He wasn't that much taller than her, but his solid shoulders could envelop her in warmth and let her close out the world for a moment. Suddenly, she lifted her head, "What day is it?"

"Thursday," he answered.

"Idiot," she gently pushed him away. "Go clean up for your dinner. I'll be fine."

"Yeah?"

"Yeah." She walked over and poured herself a glass of wine then moved to the couch. "Say goodbye to me in the morning." She smiled at him full of love and he visibly relaxed a little even though he hadn't realized that he was tense. "One way or another. You don't need to actually find me." She gave him a sly smile.

He chuckled. "Ok. Love you." He headed out the door.

"Love you, too." She watched him walk out the door, then she dropped her head back against the couch and let her eyes close. She swirled the wine gently in her glass even though it had no need to aerate. It was just soothing. She began to sip and ponder, trying to piece together any little nuance that might help.

Arichel knew the next step. She knew who she had to reach out to. But, she needed the wording just right before she even began. The good thing was, that party also knew she would be reaching out. They would know what was going on. They might or might not care, those little aloof, irritating beings with such a sense of superiority for such tiny sprite bodies. So, knowing what she would need they might already be scouting for her. Or, they might not. That wouldn't actually affect their price at all. In that, they were fair. They were very fair, and absolutely drew the hardest bargains that any world had ever known. Even the dragons didn't parley with them if they could help it, or the treas. That was saying something.

Arichel drained her glass, then stood to pour another. Hesitating, she carried the full carafe over to the couch. Just as she was setting it down, a doily appeared on the side table. "Thank you," she murmured.

The lights flickered briefly in response. Then, a plate with buttered bread, cheese, strawberries and shaved steak appeared beside the wine. She sighed, "Hmm. Yes, I should have that too. Thank you."

In response the flames kicked up a touch, the lights dimmed the slightest bit to a warmer tone, and a pen and notebook appeared on the table in front of her. Also a little wastebasket. Clearly, the house knew that she would need a few drafts and sustenance. Arichel chuckled with delight. "You are a delight, House. Thank you." Then, as an afterthought, "Make sure the others eat, too, please."

***

True to his word, Adovey messaged her in the morning, which House showed her in the mirror as Arichel brushed her hair. They would both return to the mortal world today, but she would leave early enough to begin the school day, and he would go directly to his job site.

It was always a little odd that time passed normally here, and everyone knew that she wasn't present, but the parallel world just didn't register her absence. It wasn't that she was missing, it wasn't that her role didn't get done, it was just that she wasn't even needed or missed when she wasn't there.

Someone before her had noticed that trend and tried to just use it as a vacation home then. Complete debauchery when he was there. There was a loose theory that the world had almost collapsed because of him. Certainly, there had been solar flares, storms to kick your ass, and a polarity switch. He had sort of fallen into a philanthropic hobby and suddenly all the natural disasters stopped their unnatural frequency. Sure there were still storms and wildfires, but it was normal again. The day he pondered giving up his good deeds and going back to being a playboy, there were three reported solar flares. He kept volunteering after that. The worlds seemed strongly tethered ever since.

Arichel walked down the hallway of the school. Past the Art Room where the staff meeting had been so abruptly ended last time she was there. *How did that end?* she wondered. There was strange magic that the universe used to bind the worlds together and prevent gaps. She often wondered how it worked. The staff meeting was completely interrupted by her being "invited" to a Death Duel, but what did the people remember? Did they all just have a feeling of "all was right in the world" and no real memory of the end of the meeting and what hadn't been covered? Who knew.

"G'morning," she said at large as she walked into the resource room with the three adults sitting and prepping. She dropped her bag at her desk, then headed back out to the girls' bathroom. Not the staff bathroom, it was too far and she would only have moments before the students arrived. Her next break would be hours away. Welcome to public school on earth.

On the way back to the classroom she stood in the Humanities door. She gave a nod to the teacher, "I want to talk to you later, when we both have time." She saw a look come over his face, like someone remembering the glimpse of a dream.

He nodded back, as he finished walking to the exterior door to let the first students in. They would find each other later.

Arichel's school day went as normal. Her students came in as a giggly or a half asleep bunch. Middle schoolers are a special breed and Arichel loved their moody silliness.

After Homeroom, art class began the day which was a nice ease in for her. A few students needed directions repeated and broken down, but she didn't need to instruct at all. Mostly she could talk about how she liked a student's color choices or shapes, and find little ways to build their confidence.

Math class required more work and was followed by science class. In these classes the lead teacher explained and Arichel had her group that needed the extra explanations. Often they understood the base concepts but they had no idea that they understood. Her task was usually to ask them questions and then say, "Now write that down. Exactly what you told me."

"Huh?"

"You just told me the answer. Look," Arichel would reread the question out loud, rephrase it while pointing at the parts of the question, "and you just told me why and how. So write it down."

"That's it?"

"Uhhuh."

Break times and lunch were just silliness most of the time, with a few bouts of middle school drama, gossip being nipped in the bud, and ridiculous displays of athleticism. Arichel loved the fact that the school day ended in Humanities, by far her strongest subject. Largely, she worked with the same small group of students as earlier, but again she could prod any of the students along. This subject teacher was a veteran and had an excellent grasp of students' abilities and willingness which are not necessarily the same.

He gave her a pensive look when they entered his room, and she gave him a quick grin back. "You have some 'splaining to do." He told her with a grin.

She relented to a more serious smile. "Yeah."

The students began with 20 minutes of silent reading of any book they liked. This meant Arichel actually had about 10-15 minutes of time to herself once they were settled. She had been checking her messages throughout the day, but now she could check email. A few prophecies had been forwarded to her. After reading the first bit of fairytale nonsense she decided to wait on reading the others. It wasn't like there was going to be a giant clue that was obvious in them or she would have already been informed of that. She left them in the in-box.

She moved on and replied to a few quick messages, including the one from the Magmellians agreeing to receive a formal message from her. The prickly bunch. She had sent a specially worded missive to them to ask if they would receive a message. A bit convoluted but it kept everything formal. Arichel had already been through several drafts of her formal letter request, and would finalize it this evening and have it sent. She was hoping they would respond quickly to her, but one never knew. Humanities class moved into project work, which Arichel also loved.

No one could say that these days seemed pivotal. Nothing about Arichel's actions held the worlds together. Yet, if she didn't go through this routine, or something similar, a rift happened. As that rift between these parallel worlds grew, then the worlds began to destroy themselves.

Adovey had texted to ask how her day was going. He complained (albeit good naturedly) about fabricating and aligning the pieces of the hydro plant he was working in. Riv had checked in, but really had nothing to report. That was really what most of her messages had been throughout the day. Back in homeroom for the end of the day, Arichel realized how tense her shoulders were.

As her students headed to the bus and parent pick up, she slipped out of the room and went down to the teacher's "lounge". The lounge aka "staff room" was a table and chairs, and a small table with coffee and tea items. Arichel made two cups of Earl Grey and grabbed two packets of sugar, unsure how Rhuvac drank his. Amidst little snippets of small talk she brewed the tea with the kuerig ® which was not ideal. She carried it down the hall and ducked back into the Humanities room, handing a cup to him and proffering the sugar packets as well. "I didn't know how you take it."

"Hey, thanks!" he said, but shook his head to the sugar.

Arichel leaned back against a table and waited for the students to leave, lost in thought about approaching the Magmellians.

"What the hell happened?" broke her thoughts.

Arichel gave a rueful laugh, "Huh. Yeah, that."

Rhuvac arched an eyebrow, but waited for her to speak.

"So most people don't even remember events like that. Nor do mortals even seem to notice when I'm not here days at a time." She paused and let it seep in. He would catch the term "mortals" and do some quick inferring.

"Yeah mortals," continued Arichel "of which you are and I am not. How's your understanding of parallel worlds?"

"Madeline L'Engle style?" he asked

"Yeah, close enough. That or Dr Who-ish."

"Hmm." Very noncommittal, he sipped some tea.

"Let's pretend you believe. Let's pretend you believe that I was born on another plane or another world coexisting with what you call Earth. Let's agree that there are certain ... strands that keep those worlds tethered. Those strands are what keep the worlds tethered and keep them from destruction."

"Uhhuh. And you are charged with keeping those strands safe?" he asked.

"Kinda," she smiled. "I am one of the strands."

"OK," said Rhuvac. "Let's just say this all makes sense and you're not insane, and that you are some deity holding together two worlds."

"I'm definitely not a deity," countered Arichel.

"Ok. Whatever you are, you have special skills. Even if swordfighting were common, you clearly have some political sway, too."

"Yes." Arichel decided to keep it simple. Really, she wasn't even sure why she was having this conversation. But she respected Rhuvac and had a feeling that honesty was best in this case. He might be convinced he had experienced a strange dream, but it would niggle at him every time he saw her. Better to bring it out and examine it, she figured.

Rhuvac sat down and nodded for her to do the same. "Start at the beginning."

"Short version, yeah?" suggested Arichel. "We can do a more detailed later, but I'm not spending hours explaining millennia of history of both overlapping worlds." He nodded agreement.

"Simplistically there are two parallel worlds. We know they are intimately connected and when those bonds are forgotten or not cared for the worlds begin to self destruct. As long as there are strands actively connecting the worlds, certain families connecting lives in both worlds, then everything continues as normal."

"Ok," he nodded with understanding.

"Think of all the fantasy fiction you have read, and know that it is highly influenced by the people and creatures of this other world. Time gets a little convoluted between the two, but generally passes at the same rate in both places, handy really, except that mortals overlook a lot."

"You keep saying mortals. But you're not?"

"No. I'll jump over the bad jokes about never asking a lady's age. I'm 43 here, but 711 there. Both are middle aged," she added to his raised eyebrows. "There's a few of us that travel back and forth. A day here is a day there, but we don't age the same, so our roles here change. But also there's some enchantment too, so the mortals never seem to realize if we're gone for days or weeks at a time. When did you see me last?

Rhuvac answered quickly, "Yesterday, in class." Then he pondered it more.

"Or maybe, no, it was..."

"Don't worry about it." Arichel interrupted. "It was almost a week ago, but you aren't supposed to remember that. There's this veil that hides the differences, sort of. Something that allows you to see through it, but not be able to catch the details."

"Huh."

"Yup," Arichel laughed out loud. "Alright, do you want to ask me questions?"

"Well I, uh, yeah." Rhuvac was actually taking this in stride very well. "So the duel? It was real?"

"Yes," she answered simply. Simple answers were the best way to move forward quickly. But sometimes simple still needed a few more details. "It's a little complicated, but he felt that the fate of the other world rested on his choices, which included the duel. It's a fight to the death or other agreement by the two parties." Rhuvac nodded and Arichel continued. "I won, I could have dealt a killing blow. But he is an excellent leader of his country and I would rather have him in an alliance."

"Friends close and enemies closer?"

"No, he's a friend, not an enemy. We have known each other a long time and I trust that he has good reasons for the choices he makes. It would have been a great loss to many countries to lose him. He's a good man."

"Hmm," pondered Rhuvac. "MacKerrit?"

"Huh," softly laughed Arichel. "Yeah, I didn't expect to see him at the duel. There are a number of people that can travel between these parallel worlds but who do not bind them. MacKerrit is one. He's a shrewd politician. He's an excellent leader and he's a friend."

"He's IRA. Do you know how much damage they have caused?"

"Do you know what the group was before it was the IRA? MacKerrit is as old as I am. Actually, older. He has been leading his people and protecting them as best he knows, for almost his entire life. He grew up doing it and he will die doing it. We may not agree on each other's tactics. But I respect him and the choices he has made for his people at large, for centuries."

"If you know him so well, why was your little group surprised?"

"Fair question," Arichel nodded. "Politics are murky at best. Captain wasn't surprised. If the rest of my Inner Court had been here, they would not have been surprised."

"That's right!" he exclaimed. "You're a queen?!"

"Ummhmm. I am. I was born into an ancient line of hereditary leaders of Aegnya as well as the Fae, thus uniting the two realms for as far back as modern history goes. We can get into the political maps later. Yes, I am a queen.

"What other questions? We both need to leave soon."

"The scars on your back?"

"Hmm," she bit the inside of her bottom lip. "Yeah. 711 years is a long time to collect scars. I probably have more scars than not. But the striking ones on my back are from battles and before that, training. Maybe a few stupid choices and games, too." She chuckled at herself, then continued seriously. "There is evil in the world. Both worlds. And it's not typically a scary monster hiding under the bed. It's evil people doing evil things. They have to be stopped. Sometimes it's an easy sting operation to gather evidence and arrest them. Sometimes it's...not.

"The veil works both ways, too. While it clouds the minds of mortals against discrepancies to how you understand the rules of the world, it also blurs the technological share between worlds. There is a huge leap of technology in this world that doesn't exist in the other. Laptops, cellphones, internet? Yeah, no. Libraries and messengers is where it is at."

"Medieval?"

"No, well, sort of. More Renaissance, but not. That's an oversimplification. However, a duel fought by swords and magic is exactly fitting. But the rules binding that duel between the worlds are more complicated than anything I've dealt with in a long time."

"Magic? Spells and wizards?"

"Oh yes. Hogwarts and Percy Jackson, and so much more. Ever read Zodiac Academy®? I forget the authors, there are two of them. It's a fairly recent series."

"Uhuh."

"Read one; it won't take long, It's a simple YA. It's a good series, but a little graphic to keep in the classroom here. It does have an-a surprisingly accurate description of reality. I mean, it's missing a ton, but as far as I know they wrote it as complete fiction."

***

Arichel and Adovey spent three more days in the mortal world of Earth, solidifying and repairing the binding with their presence. Adovey at least felt accomplished as the hydro plant was resuming its full capacity. Arichel was straining at the bit, worrying about missing children and strange dreams of cliffs coming alive with falcons or fields of flowers hiding small winged creatures.

Chapter 5 - The Plague

"You know that Billy Joel song, "Downeaster Alexa" or something like that? The one about the captain from New England who is dirt poor with a family who needs him to support them, but he has to travel farther and farther to catch the fish? I think that's us." Arichel was venting a little. She really felt like this was not the time she wanted to be responsible for holding two worlds together. She wanted to be actively solving the mystery of: *Where the **Fuck** were the missing children?!*

MacKerrit wasn't nearly as upset about her "lost time", but then again *he* could freely move about whenever he wanted to, with no universeunraveling consequences.

"Alright Lass," began MacKerrit until Arichel snorted in his ear through the phone. "No? I'm not supposed to call ye, Lass? Alright then, Your

Almighty Royal Highness Yourself."

Arichel laughed some more, which she sorely needed and MacKerrit probably knew this. "Yeah," she giggled, "ye ken call me, Lass. You're probably the only one, though."

"Right, then *Lass*," said MacKerrit again, "I get the onerous task ye have. I can't serve your time for ye, but we can work together here. Ye said ye have your seers and such scrolling through the ancient Aegnyan prophecies. Let me scroll through Earth's mythologies. As far back as we know and for as long as we remember, these two worlds have been connected, it wouldn't be a far stretch that some prophecies came here as myths and fairytales, eh?" "Damn." Arichel was silent for a moment. "Shit, you're right. It would be no different than the fairytales of ents and fairies, mermaids and vampyres."

"Right."

"Yeah. But there are literally hundreds of thousands of myths, fables, oracles, fairytales-"

"Aye, but I have a head start already. Ye see, I have this lovely library, with a trove of cataloged mythies."

"Mythies?" she asked, eyebrow raised, not that he could see it.

"Aye, lass, there's a bit of story, a bit of myth, and a bit of anthologies of lies, but "lies" seems rude."

"Uhhuh," Arichel was almost completely lost, but willing to keep listening. MacKerrit had a habit of being confusing as all hell until all of a sudden it all came clear. Kinda like that painter with the "happy, happy little trees". All of a sudden his bits and strokes came to life with just a "happy dab a yellow here" and voila, a gorgeous landscape.

"Ye see, Lass, I've had a little time to create a fairly large library and I happen to like comparing myths and fables to history and seeing how many fairy tales seem rooted in what I personally know to be true." MacKerrit sounded like he was describing a perfectly normal hobby. But then again after several centuries, books probably were his old friends as mortal humans had a distressing habit of dying and being upset if you didn't also.

"Ok, so you have a head start. I can still have Jarrandon or someone, come help you, he loves puzzles."

"Aye, Lass," Arichel could hear the smile in his brogue. "I'll let you know when I think I'm close to something, although it may be a wee bit of nothing, but I'll let ye know when I need more eyes."

"Alright, MacKerrit," she said, ready to end the call, "and MacKerritt?"

"Yeah?"

"Thank you."

"Of course."

Arichel ended the call, and got ready to transition back to Aegnya.

***

"A message just came in," said Lath, handing off an opened letter. "It's from the Milliner down the street.

"The what now?" asked Arichel, knowing that she knew the term, but couldn't place it.

"The hat sewer, or knitter, or hat former, or whatever the hell he does!" Lath was acting short tempered, and not like his normal, jovial self.

"OK, easy now. I forgot what a milliner was," said Arichel, placing a hand on his arm and sending cooling thoughts his way. "That's not the bee up your ass though. What's wrong?"

"Read it." Lath bit out the words and then stalked over to the side board. The house was gently placing ice into the glass of whiskey for him. As he grabbed the whiskey glass and gulped some down, a frosty glass of beer appeared with a thick head of foam on it. Lath growled something, and Arichel decided House understood it was supposed to be thank you. If House could understand her, it could probably understand Lath.

She unfolded the letter in her hand and skimmed it. "Shit." She dropped to the floor; her legs folded under her. "Shit."

Lath grunted.

She read it again. "We need everyone here."

"Yut," Lath grunted, "assuming you mean our small group and not 'everyone'."

"Obviously." Arichel's mood now matched Lath's. A glass of red wine appeared beside her. "Thank you." The lights pulsed.

"I was just calling them when I felt you coming in." Lath sat heavily in an overstuffed chair, and covered his eyes with his hand. "They're on their way."

At that moment, Riveya came through the door. Her smart ass remark about being summoned died on her lips as she read the mood of the room. The front door slammed and it felt like Captain's energy had entered the house.

Shortly, everyone had gathered in the sitting room. Except Kribell, she was a half day's travel and sent word to start without her. The letter was passed to each person as they came in. Somber was too light to describe the mood.

"That son of a bitch-" began Adovey, not for the first time.

"Hold up," said Captain. "I'm right there with you wanting to tear his head off for kidnapping our children for some petty vanity, but let's check our facts."

Lath growled. "How much more obvious do we need? He's offering to pay her for the children so he can use them to labor in his mines for some damn youth elixir!"

Adovey's face grew darker, and his teeth were grinding, but he didn't say a word. He saw what Captain was pointing out.

"Aye. Rather convenient isn't it. A letter just happened to be dropped right here in the capital, and that offers to buy children to labor in the mines. He even signs his name." Captain didn't bother to phrase it as a question.

Lath swore vehemently in three languages combined and threw his glass into the dancing flames in the fireplace. The flames whooshed high and a cloud of smoke whoomped into the room, but was immediately fanned back into the fireplace and up the chimney. Lath jumped up and began pacing the room. "Damnit!"

"Indeed." Jarrandon hadn't said much yet. "We need to investigate this as if it is absolutely, *Stupidly,* true, but we need to also look at it as a possible set-up. We need to talk to the hatmaker."

"I'll send for him," Lath agreed, "but first let me get this picked up." He strode over to the fireplace and began picking up the large pieces of glass that had hit the back bricks so hard that they had bounced out upon shattering. House floated over a trash can and lifted the slivers up from the carpet, depositing them into the trash. Lath finished the larger pieces then left to send a message.

"We need to look at all three possibilities," continued Jarrandon. "Like I said, we need details from the hat maker, but we also need to act like we think this is true and begin investigating the mines, but we also need to investigate this as a set-up to frame Dafang."

"For now, we don't tell anyone about this," added Captain. "We neither want to slander him, nor do we want to lose our advantage if it is true."

"What about the hatmaker? He'll talk won't he?" asked Riv. "Every shop owner gossips."

"Kill him." Adovey was still angry and wanted direct action.

"No," argued Jarrandon. "Even after we know what he knows, we don't kill him. We use him to see if more information can be gathered."

"Silence is golden. Can we pay him off?" asked Arichel

"Someone can always pay more."

"No one can pay more than me," said Adovey sardonically.

Lath came back into the room. "He'll be up after his shop closes."

Arichel raised an eyebrow, "Oh he will, huh? After?"

"Yeah, his assistant is ill today."

"Uhhuh," Arichel finished her glass of wine and stood.

"Well, if he's too busy to come here, certainly I can make the time to go to him."

"Arichell-" called out Riv.

She paused and turned to look.

"I know I'm hardly the one to suggest being...*nice*," said Riv, "But we do need to have him alive to get answers."

"It's fucking *children*, Riv," fumed Arichel. "He will talk to me now. And if he can't come here, I am happy to accommodate him with a meeting at his shop."

"Uhhuh," said Riv. "Alive. We need him alive and speaking. Play nice."

"Yeah." Arichel spun on her heel.

Adovey and Captain met Arichel at the doorway. "We'll be back," said Adovey to the room.

The wind grabbed the door and slammed it open as Arichel, Adovey, and Captain entered the Milliner's shop. The shopkeeper's face blanched. The trio didn't say a word, but came in and stood by the counter to wait while the milliner finished with the customer. She took one look at the three of them and said, "You seem to have some other pressing business. I can come back tomorrow."

The milliner was about to argue, but Adovey cut him off. "That would be perfect. Thank you, ma'am." The poor woman scooped up her belongings and hurried out of the shop.

As soon as the door closed, Arichel strode forward to the milliner. Behind her, on their own accord the blinds closed, the "open" sign flipped to "closed" and the air fairly crackled with angry energy. "I understand that your assistant is out and you were too busy to respond to our summons. So We have come to You."

"Um, I'm um. I'm sorry, m'Lady," stumbled the nervous milliner. "An error, a misjudgement on my part."

"Umhmm."

"Yes, I apologize. I should have just closed my shop and not wasted your time coming here." He scurried to a curtained doorway. "Please won't you come in. I'll make tea."

"No," said Captain.

"Of course, right through here-wait. No?" The milliner practically shifted direction mid-word.

"No. We'll talk right here."

"Oh, of course." The milliner dry washed his hands then squeezed them together.

Archel took a deep breath through her nose and reigned in her anger. "I'm sure we can just have a quick conversation." She smiled at the milliner to put him at ease. "We really just have a couple questions for you."

The milliner visibly relaxed, perhaps mistakenly thinking everything had been that easily forgiven.

"Of-Of course, M'Lady." He nodded eagerly and moved back towards them.

"Just tell us about the note you found," directed Captain.

"Of-of course, m'lord." The milliner took a deep breath.

"Like I said in my message that I sent with the note. I found the note on my floor and thought you would want to see it."

"You just happened to find it?" asked Adovey.

The milliner started to nod, as Captain said, "Just tell us what happened from the beginning."

"Yes," nodded the milliner. "Ok, um. So this morning was rather busy. It often is at the beginning of the week as everyone is thinking about the parties that they went to or that they will be going to."

Adovey made a *hurry up* motion with his hand.

"Yes, well anyway, it was busy and my assistant was out, so I really didn't have a chance to straighten up much during that rush. Once Mrs. Millheart and her daughter left, I finally had time to straighten the shelves and sweep. That's when I found the note on the floor, but just under the shelf there." He pointed vaguely to the side.

"After Mrs. Millheart left?" repeated Adovey.

"Yes, she and her daughter were the last two to leave," answered the milliner eagerly.

"Who else was here?" asked Arichel.

"Yes, well several people, M'Lady."

Captain growled out, "Which shelf was it under?"

The milliner hurried over to the shelf with berets on it. "Right here, m'lord." He used his foot to point under the corner of the lip of the shelf. "And, I'll um, I'll write you a list of who was here. But there was a couple I didn't know."

"Does that happen often?" asked Arichel. "Buyers you don't know?"

"Well, yes and no." The milliner gave an apologetic smile. "Often people come in that I don't know, but most of my sales are to people I know or families I have sold to for a long time."

"I see," Arichel replied. "That list would be good. Maybe you could write a short description of the people you didn't know." She moved as if to examine hats while he scrambled to begin the list.

***

Walking back to the house, they spoke quietly.

"It could have been dropped by anyone in the shop this morning. Mrs Millheart is a sweet elderly woman who forgets her own name. Her daughter is hardly any younger. I doubt either of them have children available to sell."

"Did you notice the hats on that shelf?"

"Hmm, berets like Dafang wears."

"Uhhuh."

"But it wasn't him there buying hats, so is that just coincidence?"

"More importantly, did you look at the floor under the shelf?"

They looked at Adovey blankly. "The floor?" asked Arichel. "It was wood."

"It was dirty," replied Adovey.

"Yeah. People track in a lot of dirt at this time of year."

Adovey shook his head. "The shelves were perfectly organized but the whole floor was filthy." Captain's face took on a light of understanding.

"So?" Arichel's face was confused. "I don't see-oh. He was sweeping."

"Right, he said he found the note when he was sweeping. That floor hasn't been swept today."

"Maybe he was just starting and found the note which stopped him."

"Maybe," agreed Adovey. "Or, maybe he's lying."

Later, back at the house, Jarrandon and Arichel were chatting alone. "You have to go back." He knew the stubborn look on her face, and the set of her shoulders. Her clenched fists sealed the picture of frustration. "It's a plague that can destroy the world. You have to go back."

"Fuck."

"Is that an offer?" he asked more to make her laugh than expecting a fun interlude.

"Fuck me."

"Mmmhmm."

Arichel made a face and laughed mirthlessly. "Couldn't a catastrophe in one world be enough?"

"You know the worst part?" Jarandon asked.

"Umm, missing children?!"

"Yes, ok." He grimaced, then came behind her and slipped his arms around her waist, "I *meant* the worst part about the plague on earth?"

"What." She didn't even form it like a question. She was cranky as all hell.

"It seems," he began, then he nibbled on her ear. "It seems that this plague originated in some Chinese lab with someone who wanted to create a biological warfare weapon." He slipped his hands up under her shirt and rubbed between her shoulder blades where the stress headache started. She slumped forward to give him better access. He slipped her shirt off and massaged her shoulders. "The good news is that they succeeded beyond their wildest expectations."

"Fanfuckingtastic," she mumbled.

"No," he turned her around, and continued massaging her shoulders.

Against her lips he said, "I'd rather fuck you."

Her lips met his with the comfort of centuries and her arms slipped around his neck. He did know how to make her smile.

"Stop," he whispered.

"What?" she pulled back to ask.

"Stop, you're tensing up again. Stop thinking about it." His thumb slipped under her waistband, just beside her pelvic bone.

She couldn't help it, she moaned against his lips. That just turned him on more. He pushed her backwards until his bed hit the back of her knees. They sunk down, his arms caging her in place, not that she was trying to escape. Her hands deftly undid his belt, but she struggled with the button of his pants. He helped her unfasten the button. He groaned as she reached her fingers in to rub his hardened cock. He undid her pants with far less trouble and slipped fingers in to tease her clit and stroke deeper in as she grew wetter.

They took their time, kissing and licking each other, releasing stress for each other. Then, she shifted over and pushed against his shoulders to push him aside. Following her lead, he lay down on his back and she leaned in across his thigh, one hand gently pulling at his balls, while her other hand grasped his cock and held it by her lips. She licked and teased the tip as he softly moaned again. She encircled the head with her mouth, pressing her tongue hard against the shaft just under the head where it was so sensitive. Slowly, she slid her mouth as far down as she could and sucked hard, pulling back. A few strokes like that and he groaned and pushed her away onto her back. She laughed low while he rolled over onto her and sank his belly against hers. More deep kissing, his tongue thrusting against her and then her tongue teasing his lips, and sliding back and forth against his tongue.

He lifted his body up and moved lower. He kissed and nibbled down her neck, cupping and gently squeezing first one breast and then the other. Lower still, he gently bit and licked her nipple. She spread her legs wider, pulling her knees slightly up, she raised her hips up to meet him. Gently he teased her, sliding his cock slowly in until he was buried deep. She laughed again, she knew he was teasing her, and she raked her nails against his back and shoulders. He pulled back and thrust again, moving faster and harder. She rose and thrust her hips to meet him, grinding against each other and pulling back.

He pulled his face back to look in her eyes. She grinned, then reached forward and licked against his throat where she could see and feel his pulse. She sucked quickly against his neck, enough to tantalize the nerve endings, but not enough to leave a mark. Their lips found each other again and slowly they brought each other to climax. He pulled back, paused, and then thrust deep. Then, he collapsed down onto his elbows and against her. They breathed hard against each other, and the sweat that had slicked their skin before, offered prickling cooling to their skin now.

"Give me a moment, then a bath?" Jarrandon asked, his head still on her chest.

"Yeah, that sounds good."

House began running hot water into the deep tub in the next room. Steam and lightly scented oils began to slowly waft into the room.

She slipped out from under him and walked into the other room. His eyes followed her. Still, after centuries, he thought she was one of the most sensual people he knew. She stepped into the hot, soapy water and closed her eyes. The heat soaked into her bones and eased some more of the tension from her shoulders. She felt Jarrandon come into the room, and heard him slip into the huge tub. She had seen hot tubs on earth smaller than this tub. She might feel guilty about the waste of water, but she knew House filtered it and then pumped it out to large cisterns in the garden. It wasn't wasted. And besides, it felt sooooooo good.

They sat for a while not talking and just soaking, almost simmering. Then they shared some random small chatter. Those things that aren't important but that are interesting.

"What do you think Kri meant, about a new toy?" asked Arichel.

Jarrandon snorted a laugh. "It could be a lover or a wild beast to tame. Aside from your husband, I think she views them the same." They both laughed.

House deposited some cold water with a few mint leaves and slices of cucumber by each of them. They both murmured their thanks.

"I wonder how old House is," pondered Arichel. "It seems like, despite its excellent state, that House has always been here. But it had to have been built, right?"

"And at what point does it change from wood and stone to an omnipresent entity?" added Jarrandon.

"And why? Why does this personality basically serve us? Obviously House has intelligence," Arichel further pondered. Then she asked aloud,

"House?"

The lights gently pulsed.

"I'm sorry I never thought to ask, but is there a written history of you that I could find?"

The lights pulsed slower.

Jarrandon said, "I think that's a 'maybe' in House-ese."

"House-ese?" Arichel snorted. "I guess that's apt. House, I'll ask it separately. Is there a written history about you?"

The lights pulsed at the normal tempo.

"Can I find this history?"

The lights hesitated and then pulsed slower.

"Hmm. Jarrandon?"

"Yeah, I'll look into it. Your Spymaster and Royal Puzzler is on it."

If House could talk, she would have told them that the secret history had been spelled and hidden centuries ago. But Arichel asking about it unlocked the spell and House was the one with the ability to reveal it.

Adovey was startled with a pop and soft thud when an ancient, blue-dyed leather book appeared beside the bed on Arichel's nightstand.

"Some reading material for Arichel?" House flickered the lights.

"Ok, thank you. He continued reclining in their bed, his ankles crossed, working on a crossword puzzle.

A knock came at the door. Adovey let his awareness out and 'saw' Kri. "Come in!" he called.

She opened the door and leaned her head in. "You should go get Jarrandon and Arichel."

Adovey looked at her questioningly.

"I'll get Riv and Captain. Another note just arrived."

"Shit."

Arichel broke off her sentence midword and looked at the doorway.

"What's wrong?" asked Jarrandon.

"I'm not sure," but she stood up and grabbed a towel.

Adovey called out as he came through the bedroom, "Knock, knock. Sorry to interrupt." Jarrandon stepped out of the tub and grabbed a towel, too. Adovey came in, hand across his eyes.

Arichel laughed, "It's ok, we're decent." Then more seriously, "What's wrong?"

"Apparently, there's another note. Kri sent me to get you, she's collecting Riv and Captain."

"Shit. We'll be right down."

"Yup." Adovey headed out of the room and downstairs.

"Damn. I intended to fuck you again."

"Raincheck apparently."

Arichel stood still and House enveloped her in a warm breeze to change her hair from wet to damp. Jarrandon skipped this step and simply got dressed. "Go ahead," Arichel said. "I'll be right down." She finished dressing, but then she stepped over to the window for a moment.

Adovey waited by the door.

Looking out, she watched the moonlight across the roofs of the city. Here and there windows were lit up and lanterns dotted the streets, but from this distance up on the hill, one could pretend they were twinkling stars below. Sometimes, the clouds were low enough or the fog was thick enough that one couldn't see the city below and she felt like she had a home alone in the clouds. Tonight, she thought about how the moonlight didn't nearly pierce the shadows. She cried inside for the fears of the missing children.

***

"There's nothing that says that you have to go to school, is there?" asked Adovey.

She furrowed her brow, thinking through all the history she knew. "We need to travel between them fairly often, but I don't think there is any particular "rule" about how we spend our time, assuming it's not complete debauchery all the time. That apparently doesn't bind worlds together."

"Ok"

"Why?" she asked.

"You have to be here on earth, but that doesn't mean you can't be working on this other problem. I mean you're amazing, but you don't know how to cure a pandemic. You being here may cure it, but it's not like your profession is going to cure it."

"No, Bub, you're right. Me going to school and sitting on my butt while my student refuses to do his work today is probably not the path to finding the cure." She twisted her neck trying to pop or stretch some kinks out of it.

"What did you have in mind?"

"The lake."

"Umm." She wasn't arguing, just thinking.

"It's gorgeous, it's going to be hot. You can think, we can bounce ideas there as anywhere else. Maybe better." He waggled his eyebrows like a suggestive goof.

"Yeah. Yeah, you're right," she laughed.

"It has to be referencing the prophecy, doesn't it?" asked Arichel. "I mean it's so close. The note says, 'The last one is dying, the challenger comes'. The line in the prophecy is *When the moment comes before the last one dies, a challenge shall usher in.*'"

"It seems like it, but is that just because we're looking for it?" asked Adovey. "If we didn't know about the prophecy, what would we think about it? It's still happening, it's just the weight of it that may be greater, but that doesn't make it easier to find. I'm babbling."

"Yeah, no, I get what you're saying," replied Arichel. "How we look for it isn't changed by whether it is prophecy or not. Someone is still dying and someone is getting ready to challenge something. BUT if we figure out the who and what, we might be closer to figuring out the prophecy."

"Exactly."

"Uhhuh," Arichel made a face. "So, who is dying?"

"I'd like to think it's someone important. Someone we can find," said Adovey.

"Yeah, that would be a helluva lot easier than some shepherd in the back woods," Arichel sighed.

The sound of the waves lapping against the sand, gave a relaxing feel to the beach. The sun was bright, the kind of brightness and heat soaking into your skin that you can feel yourself tanning - like bread browning in the toaster. A slight breeze tickled the hair, and kept the sun's heat to comfortable levels.

The great lake had a personality all its own. It was large-seven miles long, unimaginably deep, carved by a glacier thousands of years ago. Some days, the water seemed like an ancient soul trapped in the depths, angry and hiding deep in a cavern, holding back raw strength. Other days like today, it was like a happy sprite with little caps of foam breaking between the waves and dancing in the sunlight. Always, there was a sense of power beneath the surface. Every year there was at least one drowning, whether from a sunny beach or down through the ice. It was said that more simply went missing and were never reported. Some people claimed they could feel the yearning souls trapped underwater. Arichel only felt the depth of power. Adovey said he felt the haunting of all those ghosts. Yet despite this history, these feelings, it was one of Arichel and Adovey's favorite places.

"Do we collect a list of names of all those dying. A census of the dead?" suddenly asked Arichel.

"Huh?" caught by surprise, it took Adovey a moment to catch up. "Oh, to find the 'one' important death we get lists of all the deaths. That's tedious."

"Yeah."

"Uhhuh. It might work. But, how do we know which one matters?" Adovey's brow creased as he thought. "I guess it gives us a starting point, but we need to narrow it down."

"Yeah, can we eliminate anything? The line doesn't say anything about age or gender, or even where."

"I guess I assumed as the 'last one' that they would be old."

"Me too," Arichel smiled ruefully. "I feel like it will be someone old or ancient, but we don't actually know that."

"What if the prophecy is wrong?"

"Right now we have to assume that it's right." Arichel rubbed her temples again. "But it's just like the note. We have to assume it's important and that it's not. There's so many damn unknowns!"

She leaned back then on her towel, her legs slightly apart to avoid the sweaty feel of hot skin on skin. Likewise, her arms were slightly apart from her body, almost like a crime scene outline. She could feel the sun soaking in, she could imagine individual skin cells warming, then toasting, and a few burning. She was one of the lucky ones who hardly ever burned though. Even if she turned beet red today, by tomorrow it would be a warm red, and just tanned by the next day.

Adovey couldn't help but pause from their current puzzle and admire his wife. He could have had any trophy wife there was, but it was something about her that set his heart on fire. She wasn't drop dead gorgeous like a fairytale queen. She was intelligent and sarcastic, direct and stubborn. Her body had gone through all sorts of changes through the centuries, and was at her softest and least toned, now.

But he thought she was gorgeous, and if they weren't on a public beach he would drop down on top of her and show her exactly how distracting she was. As it was, they were not only on a public beach, but also a nude beach. While any state of dress, or lack there of, was allowed, there were strict expectations around anything that might be construed as sexual. Instead, he leaned back and admired her black bikini just barely covering her tits, and barely covering between her legs. He imagined it was warm, slick, and ready for him.

"Stop it," Arichel didn't even crack an eye.

"What?" asked Adovey innocently.

"Uhhuh," she snorted. "Stop staring."

"I can't help it. You're beautiful."

"You're sweet," she said, "but ridiculous." She moved her arm up over her eyes, to protect her eyelids from the glare of the sun. Stress was enough to give her a headache, she didn't need the white heat, the glare adding to it. She stretched her left leg out and brushed it against Adovey's foot. He moved his toes against her in response. Centuries would never change their connection, their comfort with each other. They stayed that way for a while, letting their minds wander and letting their subconscious work.

"Hey," Adovey suddenly said.

"I know," Arichel said at the same time. She sat up and they looked at each other, both seeing a satisfied gleam in the other's eye.

pop

Arichel blinked in surprise, but Adovey reacted faster and reached down to grab the scrolled paper. Never had they received a message like this on earth. Adovey quickly unrolled it.

Chapter 6 - A Summons

Adovey quickly read through the tightly rolled scroll that had appeared on their sunny afternoon at the beach, Adovey handed it to Arichel. Scanning through it quickly her eyes then moved back to the beginning to reread it more slowly. "Apparently we're done at the beach today."

"Yeah." Adovey finished the can he was drinking, then slipped on his crocs, making sure they were in 4-wheel drive for the short hike back to the truck.

Arichel slipped on a spaghetti strap shirt and denim shorts. She shook out and rolled up her towel, and made sure all their belongings were collected. They didn't hurry, but they didn't waste any time. When the Magmellians sent a message, you paid attention to it; when they bargained, you were even more careful than with a dragon. Never had Arichel been summoned to a meeting with them. The letter had been respectful, but the required haste was unmistakable.

***

Adovey dressed in his charcoal suit coat, blue dress shirt with the light blue tie, and khaki pants. This was one of the few occasions he would consider wearing a crown for, he really hated the thing. The coiled and intertwining gold had been woven to look like branches with small leaves. He tried to pretend the feel of it was a really heavy baseball cap.

Arichel wore a dark blue, sleeveless dress with the bodice cut low, cinched in at the waist and smoothly flowing to her ankles, but with two long slips of overlapping edges to make walking easy. Around the edges of the sleeve, bottom hem, and accenting her cleavage was intricate lace that had no pattern and yet evoked the feel of the veins of a leaf - fine lines millfoiled and flowing in organic swirls. A simple silver chain served as a belt, and silver bracelets with sapphires and emeralds, accented with diamonds, adorned both wrists and her upper arms. A silver choker with a large sapphire clung to her neck.

Her long dark hair was mostly down, but some was pulled back from her face and pulled back in a loose bun. That was held with two wooden rods, like short chopsticks, and adorned with hanging silver star charms of a moon and other galactic designs. Her crown was white gold, woven strands looking like twigs, with tall clear crystals spiking up. Between the crystals were pearls and silver filigree. At the front, above the crystals and pearls was a silver and diamond crescent moon, upturned as if ready to collect the rain and starlight.

This meeting required extreme alertness and formality. One wouldn't want to make a bargain by accident. Full court dress was expected and Arichel and Adovey could dress as the best.

Due course and much formality brough Adovey and Arichel standing before the Magmellians. Having been summoned, they stood before them, but no difference in rank was otherwise shown, no raised dias, no crowns more ornate than others, no scepters. In theory, they were all equals, but in practicality the Magmellians held themselves elite from the rest of society. When they did interact, they were known for often getting the better piece of a bargain.

"You may have noticed the large stone sculpture on your way in?" began a tall Magmellian in a long purple robe. HIs hair and beard were oiled to perfection, and his voice was as smooth as softly flowing water.

"We did," Arichel nodded. "I could see there were words carved in it and I assume it is laid out in precision, but we did not stop to examine it."

"Indeed," answered a woman with an equally smooth voice though higher pitched. Her robes were the same color as Arichel's dress. "In fact there are eight languages carved into it, and the precise layout allows it to serve as a calendar, a sundial clock, and a compass."

Adovey spoke, "That's impressive. The mathematics must be remarkable to allow the layout to accomplish calendar, clock, and compass. The eight languages explain that?"

"Why no," another man spoke, this one dressed in crimson robes and with a voice more akin to water moving over rapids. "The eight languages are instructions to rebuild society following an apocalypse."

"We wish to avoid," the woman interrupted, " a need for the Guardian Stones to be used."

Arichel and Adovey somberly agreed. "These *Guardian Stones* are good to have, but agreed, we wish not to ever need them."

"We believe," the green robed man spoke again, "that you do believe this and that you are working towards this as are we."

"We note also," added a second woman, her voice clear like the first woman's, but dressed in a sunflower yellow robe, "that you strive to hold the balance between these two parallel worlds."

"I do," agreed Arichel, unsure why this was being brought up in this conversation. As far as she knew, those bonds were secure.

"Yes, and you have done well with the balance." The green robed man nodded and gave her an almost-smile.

"So we agree that you need to know of the other world." The yellow robed woman spoke again.

Arichel was speechless for a moment as she felt like the floor tipped away from her. Adovey stepped close to her as he knew her world had just rocked.

"Uh, say what?" Forget poise, Arichel was floundering with this idea. "Who lives there? Why didn't we know?"

"You didn't need to know," said the green robed man.

"But now you do," continued the blue robed woman. "Do what you will with this knowledge."

"Ask the dragons for the gate." The crimson robed man spoke last.

Suddenly Arichel and Adovey were blinking in the sunlight, outside by the sculpture. Adovey shaded his eyes, looking more closely at the sculpture.

"The Guardian Stones, huh?"

"Yeah," breathed Arichel, holding out a hand to touch the stone and catch herself. She wasn't dizzy so much as overwhelmed. Her hand against the cold, hard marble, that felt just like marble should, immediately grounded her.

"We need to talk to the others."

"Yes," agreed Arichel, "but first..." She walked around the sculpture until she found a language she could read. She recognized some of the others but she wanted easy reading to be sure of her understanding.

The first instructions were about clean water, shelter, food, and some medicinal plants. Then, some descriptions of different races and their strengths of knowledge - a list of experts. Then, government and representation structures. Finally, lines of music, followed by mathematical equations, and an illustration of the sky.

Arichel and Adovey held hands for a moment looking. When they were ready they traveled back to their home in Aegnya. "Shit, another world," breathed Arichel as they left.

***

"What do you mean there was no bargain?" asked Riveya. "Of course there was. The Magmellians never do anything without an agreement."

"No, we didn't ask for anything, they didn't require anything. They actually spoke quite plainly, not a riddle like sometimes."

"What *exactly* did they say?" asked Lath.

Jarrandon sat there with his chin cupped in his hands and only his eyes swiveling to each speaker. If this had been a cartoon, one would see into his head and there would be a whole series of gears and belts whirring at blinding speed with smoke rolling out. But it wasn't a cartoon and only his eyes swiveled. Captain was speechless, usually of few words, but utterly speechless until he said, "Good Godess, a whole world we never built defenses for. Imagine if they attack, we'd be clueless until it was too late."

Kri laughed dryly, "Our defenses aren't all specific. I think some of them would work regardless of where the intruders call home."

Captain harrumphed.

"As I was saying," said Lath in an exasperated tone, "What exactly did they say?"

"I don't remember verbatim-"started Arichel.

"I do," interrupted Adovey. "First, there was an explanation of their

Guardian Stones-"

"Guardian Stones?" interrupted Jarrandon, speaking for the first time. "They're real?"

"Yes, but not important at the moment. Brilliant though," answered Adovey. "They explained the Guardian Stones to lead into the fact that they are trying to avoid a world apocalypse, as are we. They also praised Arichel for holding the two worlds together. But here is where it gets interesting. They said, and I quote, 'So we agree, that you need to know of the other world.' That was the chick in the yellow dress."

"Robe," corrected Arichel.

"Whatever. Then Arichel asked who lives there and why doesn't anyone know about it?

Then, Mr. Green Robes said, 'You didn't need to know.'

'But now you do,' said Ms Blue Robes.

'Do what you will with this knowledge,' said Ms. Yellow Robes. And 'Ask the dragons for the gate,' by Mr Red Robes.

"Then whoosh, we were translocated outside next to their Guardian Stones."

"So the dragons know," mused Kri. "Anyone feeling draconic tonight? No, no one? I guess that means me, I do like fire whiskey so I guess that's closest to breathing fire." She looked at the glass in her hand and then swallowed it down. She blinked, House had already refilled it. She smiled her thanks.

"Not yet, though," cautioned Captain.

"Oh really," she quipped, dripping with sarcasm, "I shouldn't just walk into the dragons and serve myself up for their evening snack. Gee, how disappointing."

"They don't always eat people."

"No, just the annoying ones. That's why I'll go." Kri grinned at that, and the mood lightened slightly.

"Dinner and a plan first," suggested Jarrandon.

"I'll cook," Riv volunteered. Seeing their surprised looks, she added "Kitchen work helps me think sometimes. I think it's the slicing and dicing."

"Ok then," agreed Arichel. "I'm going to take a shower to try to loosen my shoulders and clear my thoughts."

They separated then, each to their own selfcare and pondering. Adovey and Arichel went straight through their bedroom to the bathroom. Their crowns and jewels had whisked themselves under lock and key as soon as they arrived at the house. Fine clothes were draped over a bar, to be cleaned and hung back away.

House already had the shower running with hot water, and steam slipped out from the curtain. Arichel stepped in and Adovey followed. She turned to face him, so the hot water could wash over her neck and shoulders. He leaned forward and kissed her softly, then firmly. He leaned his forehead against hers and reached around to knead her shoulders.

House had heated the shower for them, but Adovey and Arichel heated each other's blood.T he worlds might be unraveling, maybe all THREE worlds, but they needed some time just for them, to ground each other. They needed to loosen some pent up energy in the centuries old way.

Adovey kneaded Arichel's shoulders and slowly the tension loosened a little. They kissed softly with little nibbles at each other's lips. Then, with mouths open and tongues darting.

Adovey slid his hands from her shoulders down against her wet skin to her waist, and pulled her against him. Arichel's breasts pressed up against his chest, belly to belly, hips to hips. More passionately they kissed. Nipping at each other's lips, sliding tongue against tongue, teeth sometimes bumping against teeth. Kisses interrupted breathing which led to light panting. As their hands explored each other's body, little gasps escaped between their lips.

Her hand slipped down between them to grasp his manhood. Neither hard nor soft at first, it quickly grew in her hand responsive to her squeezing and slight tugging. Adovey groaned. His hands slid up to cup her breasts. He pulled his head back from her mouth and then brought tongue and lips to her neck. At the same time he rolled a nipple between his thumb and fingers, gently tugging. Arichel dipped her knees a little and reached further between his legs to cup his balls and gently squeeze and tug.

Andovey reached behind them and turned off the water. Arichel grabbed the two towels and handed one off to Adovey. They grinned at each other as they dried themselves off. She darted into the other room.

"Oh no you don't," he growled right behind her.

Laughing, she jumped up and spun around onto her hands and knees on the bed with him following right behind. He pushed her back and climbed over her. His hands planted by her shoulders, his knees just outside hers. He held himself up, so she reached down again to grab his cock and gently but firmly pull and slide her hand. He closed his eyes for a moment and groaned. She reached up and kissed him on his full lips. He deepened the kiss, opening his eyes, bright green today, and stared right into her. Her blue eyes sparkled as she brought her right hand to her clit, her left still rubbing him. She raised an eyebrow and he looked down between their bodies and saw that she was gently rubbing her clit with her middle finger while rubbing him.

"Yessss," he groaned. He licked his lips and stared, getting even harder in her hand. She moved her hand and lifted her hips to push up against his cock, her left hand pushing it against her clit.

He sank down on her, hips to hips, belly to belly, his weight mostly on his elbows and knees. She wiggled against him and they kissed, tongues darting between their mouths and flicking lips.

"Fuck me," she said. It wasn't an order or a question, but something in between.

He pulled back and they shifted legs so that hers were opened wide and he was between them. He slid into her slowly, deeply and pulled back. She bit her lip and held his gaze. He thrust and withdrew again, but a little faster, and she lifted her hips to meet him. The tempo increased with their passion, until it seemed a wonder that the bedframe didn't fall apart. Her fingers wandered the soft skin between his ribs and hips, her tongue licked his neck and then she lightly sucked where his pulse pounded. She moved her arms under his and up his back towards his shoulders. She pulled him down and closer as she rode him harder, grinding against him.

"Cum, Baby"

"You ready?"

"Cum."

He pulled back farther than he had been, hesitated and then plunged deep inside. They strained together, almost holding their breath, and then relaxed against each other. She rested back and he dropped his weight momentarily against her, before rolling off. Then they lay together with their arms against arms, legs against legs, and caught their breath.

"That," he said, "was nice."

She laughed at the inadequacy of the statement. "Yeah."

After a few minutes, she added, "Let's actually take a shower now and then head down for dinner."

"Go ahead, I'm mostly clean, I'll just rinse when you're out."

"Yup."

House considerately turned back on the hot water and replaced the wet towels. Walking in and seeing the fluffy, dry towels hanging, Arichel murmured, "Thanks."

Dinner conversation centered around the notes that had been found, the Magmellians' lack of bargaining and their bombshell, and ideas of what to do next.

"Do we send an official envoy to this other world, or do we visit covertly?"

"I think we do both," replied Jarrandon.

Captain interjected, "But we don't make this public yet. Obviously not until after Kri is back with the information from the dragons, but even during the first official envoy."

"So what?" asked Arichel, "Send an introductory envoy 'Hey, we just learned you exist' and then publicly visit this new world after we make friends?"

"Exactly."

"IF we make friends."

"What do you mean 'If,' Adovey?"

"He's right." said Captain and Jarandon together.

"Mmmhmm, I see," Arichel was thinking aloud and it showed as her comments and thoughts jumped around. "They may not be friendly, hence we haven't known about them. So maybe we don't officially introduce ourselves until Jarrandon's people return."

"Yes-"

"-I'm not sending my people," interrupted Jarrandon.

"What do you mean?" asked Arichel and Lath almost at the same time.

"I'm not *sending* my people into an unknown world. *I go* with Lath and a few of my people," stated Jarrandon clearly. "Then if it seems reasonable, the Royal Ambassador visits with a very small envoy. *Then,* we announce it to the people."

"Thanks," commented Lath dryly.

"You don't think the King and Queen ought to be in the first envoy?" asked Adovey irritated. He seldom threw his title into the conversation.

"No, we don't," answered Lath.

"No," agreed Captain.

"Not yet," answered Jarrandon

"We need to assume the worst," added Captain.

"Why don't I try to add this to my charming conversation with the dragons?" asked Kri. "Not only where in the hell the gate is, but everything they can tell me about this other world."

Riv snickered, "That would be too easy."

They all laughed and some tension eased.

"Right," recapped Arichel. "Obviously Kri will charm as much information as she can from the dragons, and we should consider how much she should have to offer to buy from them when they are done freely sharing. Jarrandon, it might behoove us for you to give Kri a secret or two that she could bargain with." Jarrandon momentarily looked grumpy at that, but he could immediately see the reasoning. "Moreover, we need to talk about you being unwilling to risk my life, but happily jumping into the unknown danger yourself."

"No," agreed Lath, "we don't need to discuss that. That is exactly what our roles are here. When push comes to shove, and we are being shoved, Captain leads the armies, I am the Royal Ambassador, Jarrandon is our best spy, and we all protect the Royal Bloodline. That's you two, in case you forgot." He turned quickly to Riv and Kri, "The ladies are just as important. But ultimately our roles are to offer advice and be the final perimeter of protection around you."

"I don't like it."

"No, you wouldn't. Channel your inner Queen Eleynia or something. She's sweet and graceful on the outside and protects her home with fangs. ...So to speak."

Kri giggled, "Maybe not the best comparison considering we suspect her husband to be kidnapping children."

"No, we're investigating her husband, I don't suspect him."

"True, the investigation will clear him, or prove his guilt. Either way we need the answers, we just hope the answers are favorable."

"We NEED to find those children!"

"Trust me, Riv," promised Adovey with cold hate, "we are doing everything we can to save those children."

"Which brings up another issue," said Captain. All eyes moved to him in concern. "We need to remember these children have been through huge trauma. We need to be ready to support them, just as we would prisoners of war."

"He's right," agreed Riv. "We can't just swoop in, save them, and return them home."

Lath spoke up, "I've been having some new clothes made up for them by various guilds around the towns and the other countries' ambassadors are arranging the same. We figured either their clothes would be ragged and disgusting or they would be in some sort of foreign uniform. Either way, clean and fresh clothes from their homelands would go a long way to their peace of mind. Hot baths, clean clothes, and hot food, are the first priorities after we have them safe."

Arichel knew of these plans, they had brainstormed together. This trauma would likely affect the children and their families, for the rest of their lives. "Uhhuh, Lath and the others are also arranging with the bakers guild and farming guilds to have deliveries of fresh food available for this at a moment's notice. No one has balked, we value our children."

Riv tapped her finger against her chin, "We can create rough plans for all the physical needs: transport,medicine, food, clothes. But what about their emotional needs? Spiritual needs?'

"Yeah, that's trickier," agreed Adovey.

"The unseen wounds," added Kri.

"Not just the missing children, but their families caring for them, and their friends who didn't suffer the same way." There will be waves of problems following their return. Some kids and families will just fall back into old routines, but some will internalize all these emotions and then explode."

"Yeah." The entire group sighed sadly.

House dimmed the lights momentarily in sad agreement, too.

Chapter 7 - Envoys

Kri left early in the morning for her meeting with the dragons. She carried a gift of an immense sapphire egg, wrapped with fine Faewrought silver filigree. Despite the myths on Earth, the Fae were the finest silversmiths and could work strands as thin as spider web into intricate designs.

She also carried two sealed parchments of secrets that Jarrandon thought would be dragon-worthy, if she needed to bargain. He refused to tell her the secrets, not from lack of trust but because of the telepathic abilities of the dragons. The secrets would only be worthwhile if they were secret.

He gave her one last scroll to be used as a last resort bargaining piece. She didn't know the contents of this one either and he wouldn't meet her eyes about it. As she walked out the door, her thumb rubbed the wax seal. She contemplated opening it. It scared her because there had only been a handful of times in their entire lives that Jarrandon wouldn't meet her eyes.

"It's enchanted," Jarrandon called after her.

"Damnit." Her thumb halted. "Ass," she called over her shoulder as she walked to the traveling grounds.

"Love you, too," he laughed.

Kri found Adovey and Arichel at the grounds ahead of her. Apparently they were going to Earth for a day to confirm the ties between these worlds. It made sense, they couldn't do much here until they heard back about the trip to the dragons.

They could plan what Jarrandon should look for when he scoped out the new world, but he knew even better than they did what he should do.

Adovey stepped into the roped off square first, and then through the portal on the back side. That circular portal would carry a person to earth. Where one landed was up to the intentions of the traveler. Traveling was not a good time to let your mind wander, especially as very few spells would work on earth. Thus, it was roped off and under royal guard. No one was technically barred from using it, except for a couple misbehaving bandits every few centuries, but no one was really welcomed to it either. There were a few other portals but they were not well known. MacKerritt had another he typically used and several other royal courts had them.

Once Adovey had left, Kri looked to Arichel. She knew that Arichel had a thing about being either the first or last to travel. Something about *Guarding the Ways*. Now wasn't the time to try to find out. Arichel nodded her chin forward and Kri stepped over the ropes. But she moved to the right (outgoing) side, leaving plenty of room on the left in case anyone came traveling in at the same time. She turned to look at Arichel and winked, then she was gone.

Arichel stepped over the ropes then and moved forward. She paused for a moment feeling the energies. There were always residues from traveling. Kri's and Adovey's were the most recent. There was another, almost as fresh, which had probably been Lath when he headed out. She hadn't heard him leave the house though. There were no residues of anyone arriving recently.

Arichel thought of her other home and stepped through the lightly pulsing circle. Not even a moment later she was stepping through a doorway normally hidden behind a bookcase. She could have arrived anywhere, but the hidden room was a perfect arrival spot as it was never used so no one was likely to be hurt by a second traveler appearing in the same spot.

She quickly moved into her room and changed into jean capris and a simple t-shirt. She picked up her cell phone from beside the bed, skipping the notifications and checking the weather. Yes, capris would work. Then she began reading the notifications from coworkers and friends on her phone. After reading and responding to those, she clicked into the app for her local news station and skimmed the local headlines, then national and international.

The world was so very confused about this virus that was spreading with incredible speed. Travel between most countries was now shut down by plane, ship, or train. Cars were still crossing some borders, but the lines were incredible, and a proof of need (jobs, education, etc) was required. Rumors were running rampant whether the virus was some sort of variant that had hopped across species or whether it had been created in a lab and set free. Maybe it was even a biological weapon, or maybe it was set loose just to test the international response...rumors were crazy. Meanwhile people were uniting in fear or disbelief.

Arichel went to the school, following her normal routines. Upon checking her email, Arichel was surprised to find an update from the superintendent saying that there was the likely possibility that if the virus followed the expected pattern of spread, that schools might temporarily close. This meant that assignments, resources, and meals would need to be sent home with students. Not everyone would have internet access, so that was a consideration as assignments were developed. Realistically, not all students would even be able to complete school work as they might be watching younger students at home as parents would still need to work. Other students wouldn't complete any work because they didn't want to and would have no one to hold them accountable. The assignments shouldn't be "busy work" but nothing new could be introduced. *Well, what the fuck.*

***

That evening the Inner Circle was grouped around the dining room table waiting for Kri. They were all tired, stressed, and anxiously awaiting her return. Arichel was alternating between hard cider and coffee, one steaming hot and the other ice cold. Riv was sipping white wine and hot black tea. The men were all drinking dark, foamy beer. Captain was also drinking dark, bitter coffee. House had provided them each with meals that they enjoyed, but nothing too extravagant, seemingly knowing that they were only picking at their food while waiting for Kri. Suddenly, Arichel looked up feeling a tingle of energy at the Traveling Grounds. She didn't normally ward them, but she had tonight.

Lath saw her look up, "Is she here?"

"I think so. Someone just arrived."

They waited in silence, until they heard the door downstairs. The fact that they didn't feel any wards triggered meant that it was someone from the Inner Circle who entered. They were all able to feel the wards for the House - that was for safety's sake. But, had they all felt every time one of them came or went, they would never have been able to sleep or concentrate between the group of them, they were often on the move.

"Who was the kid who just came through the Grounds ahead of me?" asked Kri as she walked into the room. She looked fatigued, but not upset or stressed.

"What?"

"Some kid, I dunno," and then directed to House for delivering a glass of water and a glass of wine to her place at the table, "Thank you."

"I'll find out, but I don't actually care right now," said Captain.

"Right."

"So what happened?"

Kri had the full attention of everyone at the table, but still she held up a finger in the multiverse signal for "wait". She drank the full glass of water and then sat down. House refilled the glass, but Kri didn't reach for anything else. House placed a soup bowl in front of her, but it was empty.

"Good thinking, House," murmured Kri. "I'll tell you everything," said Kri.

"First a quick overview, and then we can pick apart the details while I eat."

"Reasonable," agreed Lath.

Captain had been studying Kri just as much as Adovey had. They both relaxed as they saw that Kri didn't show any signs of harm, and no more stress than traveling and politics usually caused.

"As you say."

"Yeah," Kri visibly organized her thoughts. "So it wasn't bad. In fact, it might have been one of my most successful discourses with them ever. They were expecting us and said they were about to send a representative to us if they didn't hear from us soon. It could have been you to go, Lath." She gave him a nod of respect, then turned to look at Adovey and then Arichel. "They had just learned about your summons by the Magmellians. They directed me to say 'Thank you for the sapphire gift.' by the way."

Kri was bouncing around a little, but it was almost focussed and her friends were used to it. Jarrandon bit his lip to keep from asking whether she had used his secrets. Either she would tell them at her own speed or he would find her later, he didn't want to interrupt her thoughts now. Sometimes it was the first impressions that we don't even know we have, that end up being the most important.

"So the dragons confirmed this third parallel world. Good news is that they are in charge of binding it to this world so you're off the hook, Arichel." Arichel smiled at this, but didn't say anything to interrupt Kri.

"They also said that the world is full of strife and power struggles but they were unlikely to attack us to expand."

Captain and Adovey both relaxed a little at this. "That's not quite the right translation. Draconic languages are a bit different than ours and it had to do with enlarging caves and hordes of gold, but anyway, that's the gist. They're unlikely to try to take over. However, that doesn't mean that they might not try to use us. There was the distinct implication, and I couldn't seem to nail the dragons down, that this other world has our children. It's called Losunkion, or something like that.

It has 'sunk' in the middle, but dragons don't actually speak our language. Anyway it's 'Land of the Lost.'"

"Seriously?" Arichel couldn't help herself.

"Yup," grinned Kri sardonically. "So they have the lost children, this land of the lost, but the dragons don't know why. It's probably more practical than political. They gave me a map - *they gave it* - to the three portals." House filled Kri's soup bowl then and she leaned forward to begin eating.

"Map, now," demanded Lath.

"Nope. After I eat and then we can plot the portals on our big map." She began gulping down soup, blowing on each spoonful but shoveling it in as the steam was still rolling off. Showing an unusual hesitation, House was about to drop a roll in front of Kri but then floated it over to Riv.

Riv nodded and reached out for it even as she was setting down her fork. She broke open the thick potato roll and heavily buttered it. The butter melted easily and soaked into the soft, yellow flesh of the roll. Then House deposited it from Riv's open hand to the edge of Kri's bowl.

"Thanks," muttered Kri, though to whom she was directing her gratitude was unclear.

"I know you're hungry," started Adovey "but we're going to assault you with questions now." Kri nodded. She knew they needed her information, but her belly was an empty hole. Traveling depleted energies. Conversing with dragons depleted energy. And, to make it worse, the stress of the trip had meant that she didn't eat before leaving. The dragons had offered her food, but their fare wasn't quite what she would eat, even if she did enjoy her steak rare. She had drank only water and a little wine for the whole day. "Shoot," she said, and blew on another spoonful of thick, steaming soup.

Lath began first, "The dragons freely shared information just like the Magmellians did?" Upon her nod, he muttered, "This is bad. These people... or whatever-are giving us free information to save the universe."

"Three portals are marked on your map?" seeing her nod, Captain mused,

"That shouldn't be so hard to guard. Maybe makes your job easier too, Jar." "Did they give any indication of why the children were taken?" demanded Riv. Her eyes burned, she was really pissed about innocent children being taken and used.

"No, not really," Kri shoved a bit of roll in her mouth, but hardly paused to swallow before continuing. "Draconic concepts aren't quite the same as human, but the gist was it was more about this world enlarging their treasure hoard and not anything to do with ruling power."

Jarrandon interjected, "But you should remember that part of a dragon's power or authority comes from their hoard. A lot of it is brute strength but also the unique treasures and power the treasures give them."

"So could they be held for ransom?"

"I don't think it's that simple," said Kri. "I'm not sure, but I don't think it's that political. I think they needed children for some magical purpose, something that only children can do."

"Are the children safe?" aske Riv

"I'm not sure." Kri smiled gently at Riv, "The dragons weren't sure. They said they weren't being harmed directly, but that they were being held captive and forced to work."

"Do you think the dragons have more information than what they gave you?" asked Lath.

"I'm sure they kept a kernel or two back. They always do," said Kri. "But I think they honestly believe that they gave me enough. They do want us to get our children back, in part to continue our culture's knowledge. You know how they value knowledge. But also, I don't think they want this Losunkion place to achieve the goal that they are using the children for."

There was general muttering at that. "Why don't they deal with it then? Especially since they are the binders."

"Also," Kri said, "Arichel, they told me to tell you that the plague on earth is connected. You won't be able to cure the plague, but you can help some by showing them the Hedges."

"What?" Arichel's head had started to throb as she took in all this information. She rubbed her temples and tried to crack her neck.

"The gist was, don't try to cure the world, not even your presence will do that. But some can be helped by visiting the hedges."

"Ok." Arichel blinked fast as she processed this but decided she wasn't going to take more time on that now. Not until they circled back to the connection between the plague and this other world. *Children first, plague second.*

"So the next step," Jarrandon mused, "is that we plot these portals on the map and we all learn where they are. Then my team and I scout ahead. Once I send information back, Lath can start planning official envoys, then royal envoys." Jarrandon rubbed his chin while he thought. "Don't head over until we can talk in person so I can give you nuances, but I'll start sending basic information as soon as I can."

Lath nodded, "You know what we need from military to government to the children. But also, it will help us make a favorable impression if we know some about their dress, what they value for gifts, and culture." He laughed bitterly, "You know, learn their entire social system, history, geography, government, and religion and report back in a few hours."

"Yeah," grumped Jarrandon, understanding both the jest and the truth of the statement. "I'll do my best."

"Be careful," said Kri uncharacteristically gently.

"Of course, Little Sister," he smiled at her and winked. "Always."

"Hmmm. Always?" She lifted an eyebrow.

"Hmm. Mostly."

They finished their meal in a hurry and then moved to the planning room.

Riv pulled out her map gifted from the dragons.

Chapter 8 - The Library

The next two days passed in a whirlwind of concern for Arichel as her friend and her lover was in a strange land, spying on a people they knew nothing about. Of course she worried; they all did. Since there was nothing her worrying could accomplish, she traveled to Earth to maintain the bindings. To clear her mind, or at least let her brain sort through random thoughts in an open manner, she went for a run. A jog, maybe. Maybe walking and sprints, but she called it a run.

The trails near her house were primarily designed for mountain bikers, but anyone could buy a membership and use them to bike, or run, or walk, or ski, or snowshoe - depending on the season. She had a little two mile loop that she chose to run mostly uphill. She could pound out her heart's frustrations to the beat of her feet thudding against the packed dirt. Plus, she almost never met anyone. If she did, they passed with just nods or smiles. There was no need for interactions, formal action, or any responsibilities.

She listened to the squirrels scold her, and the wind whispering through the branches. Her thoughts untangled as she went, so she could actually think coherently once she returned sweaty and tingly to the house. Her thoughts swirled through a chaotic mess of things to do and then settled on the night before.

After the Inner Court had met about the dragons, the Losunkions, and next steps, her friends had drifted away to shore up their individual plans or to grab some sleep. Arichel hadn't been able to relax. Eventually, she asked House for a mug of chai and stepped out into the gardens to feel the starlight and moonlight on her skin. The barest of a breeze kissed her face as she looked up and she breathed in the night air. Finally, she stepped back in the house, and passed through to the back. From her study, she pulled the right combinations of books and nicknacks on her bookshelf and The Library passage opened.

House had shown her this passage centuries ago when she was a little girl. It was a handy shortcut that she liked to use during the nights she couldn't sleep.

House was built on a hill overlooking the capital city. "City" was a loose term, it was more than a town but less than a city. There were maps showing the city limits, but when walking along it was difficult to see where it would change from "town" to "country". The walls were within the "city" portion, having been built centuries ago. Arichel liked the easy blend from the outer city to the country. Her house was one of the higher built houses, actually it was the highest built house, the other high built buildings were military training grounds, churches, and other "official" buildings. House seemed pretty unassuming from the front. It had a moderate yard with various flower beds around, and a vegetable and herb garden to the side. There was a small waterfall that came off a cliff face of the hill that formed a tiny trickling stream and fed a fountain just past House's iron fence. The towns folk said the water was the best tasting around. Many people traveled to the fountain daily to collect special drinking water for their families. Scholars had tested it and said that it had an extra mineral not found in the rest of the town's supply.

House was set against the hill. With the bottom foundation set back into the hill. While most people assumed this was just to give more space to the front yard, Arichel recognized this was the space of the passageways. Among these was her entrance to The Library and there was a staircase that went deeper into the hill that led to the mountain behind which held the royal vaults.

Arichel stepped into the stone passageway that was somehow warm and airy despite being a tunnel. Flames in wall sconces sprang to life and her mug refilled with steaming chai. The door swung closed behind her as she walked forward. Arichel walked deeper into the hill and down the spiraling path. These tunnels were one of the only times her fear of enclosed spaces was never triggered. Soon the path reached an end with a heavy oak door on her left, but she turned and faced the blank wall opposite. Just below the wall sconce there was a loose stone on the floor. She picked it up and fit it into a tiny indention just beside the wall sconce. The air shifted, and a humming could almost be felt below her feet as a second door shimmered into view on the blank wall. She stepped through this door once it was solid enough to open. This tunnel was different. The air was completely still and void; it felt uninhabited. The wall sconces did not spring to life and House did not envelope her in safety.

Arichel walked down the still tunnel, almost holding her breath. House had no comforting touch here. This was a space looked upon by only the energies of the universe. Gods, some called them, but older than even the concept of deities. Arichel wasn't even a speck of dust to them, maybe dust on a distant non-existent star to them. Yet when she traveled this tunnel, she knew they took notice. She felt their observations. Some watchers were bored, some were curious, some were supportive, and some waited for her to trip. She forced herself to breath and walk forward steadily. The warm chai in her hand kept her mind grounded. House couldn't protect her here, but gave her every tool it could. She walked forward.

Not soon enough, another door formed in the darkness and these entities allowed her entrance to their Library. There was no question it was a place of sacred ground. It held an energy that was neither good nor bad, but heavy. Seldom had Arichel, nor her line of ancestors, traveled to this space outside of time. She pulled open the cold, heavy door and stepped through as if she wasn't terrified with every fiber of her being.

Arichel was judged in a nanosecond that stretched across eons as she stepped through the doorway. Found worthy, the suffocating weight of judgment lifted. The light was strange, like shifting sunlight filtering through clear lake water to a clean and sandy bottom. The air was warmer, and a feeling akin to House's welcome enveloped her. It was like House but not - older and more confident, but safe and secure. The mug of chai began to steam in her hand again.

"Thank you," she murmured and ducked her head. The shimmering light grew pinker for a moment.

Light bells chimed softly to her right, and Arichel dutifully followed the sound. Soon she was at a bookcase four times her height and packed full of books ordered and organized with even more books stacked on top of those. She closed her eyes and lightly ran her fingers over the spines of the books closest to her, letting her mind reach out as she searched and shared her need. She opened her eyes as she heard a book slide out ahead of her. Jutting out from the shelf poked a book with a deep blue cover, then another poked out beyond and then another. She closed her eyes again and set out a feeling of gratitude. Another spine hesitantly poked out, and another. Arichel stepped forward to pull the books out. Another bell softly chimed, and she followed the sound. Soon she was sitting at a table, by a cheerful fire, with a stack of books, a pen, and plenty of paper.

Arichel worked for hours. Her chai would refill periodically, and at some point a plate of hard cheese and grapes materialized. As she wiped her fingers on her leg after taking a bite, a napkin appeared on her lap. "Thanks," she murmured. She was fairly confident that most librarians didn't allow food or drinks in their walls, and certainly not in with such precious pages as these. You could bet anything that she would respect the privileges she was being given.

After a couple hours, Arichel looked up and winced as pain lanced through her neck. "Ouch!" She began to rub her neck, stretched it side to side, and yawned. "What time is it, I wonder?"

The lights pulsed, but with a different rhythm. It wasn't the sure or comforting pulses she was used to, but if it were a sound she would say it was a light trilling, or the equivalent of a dog cocking his head to the side while looking at you with a confused face.

"Hmm. There isn't a measurement of time here, is there?"

The lights pulsed in answer, not quite affirmatively, but in agreement.

"Mmm, ok. There's time passing but at a different rate than elsewhere."

The lights pulsed quickly.

"I need to go back, but I'm not finished. I don't want to lose these books, but I can't just leave my stuff sprawled all over?"

The Library took care of the problem quickly. The dishes were swept away, and a woven basket materialized that was just the right size to hold the books and papers. The basket did not have any handles.

Arichel gently loaded the books into the basket, with the papers tucked under the top book. A blue pottery mug appeared nestled into the corner. Then a silver ribbon appeared over and around the basket, holding the books and papers secure. *Queen Arichel* was embroidered into the ribbon.

"Ok, then. Thank you." She stood and stretched then, and when she was ready a low chime beckoned her and she followed the sounds back to the heavy wooden exit arch. Her hand rested against the door as she asked, "I assume that the books will be ready for me whenever I might come back? For it might be several of my days before I can."

The lights gently pulsed and the door opened for her.

This time the passageway was brief, the air was cool, but not at all uncomfortable. Wall sconces were at both ends and in the middle, so while it was not bright, there weren't really any shadows either. Looking up, Arichel could see the universe of stars (despite being inside a mountain) but there was no judgment, just a starry night. She was sure that there was some enchantment that would protect the corridor from rains or storms, but tonight was beautiful.

Arichel slipped back through the House and to her bedroom.

"Everything ok?" asked a sleepy Adovey.

"Yeah, I was just doing some reading."

"You weren't gone very long," he murmured, slipping back into sleep.

She looked at the water clock and saw that indeed it was only a little past midnight. The hours in The Library had only been minutes here. Letting out a sigh of relief for the chance for actually sleeping, Arichel scooted over until her back was pressed against Adovey's warm body. His body heat soaked into her and relaxed her as she drifted off to sleep.

***

In the morning, after Arichel had almost a full night's sleep despite spending hours in The Library, she prepared to go to Earth to keep the bindings strong. Jarrandon and his party would be gone for as long as he needed regardless of where she was, she might as well keep up her responsibilities rather than miss him until he returned.

Lath was in the dining room early, too. He was drinking coffee and eating some sort of sandwich with a heaping side of bacon.

"Where'd you go last night?"

Startled, Arichel looked up from buttering her toast.

"What do you mean?"

"Where'd you go last night?" he asked again, smiling to soften the question.

"Oh, I don't know why it would surprise me that you noticed," she said. "I couldn't sleep so I walked about the garden with some chai to settle my brain."

"It didn't work." He said it not as a question and then took a ginormous bite of his sandwich.

"No," answered Arichel as a cheesy and vegetable omelet appeared in front of her and then a small plate with crispy bacon. "There's so much going on and so many strands to try to tie together." Lath nodded. "The dragons told us the Earth plague is connected so I'll go there today, but all I can really think about is Jar and this new world stealing our children."

"He'll be ok."

"I know," she laughed bitterly. "Except, we don't know that. We know nothing about it there or the people there, except that they aren't above stealing children, so I don't know he'll be fine."

"Right," Lath held her gaze, "but he's good at what he does. The best. He'll be ok. And if he's not, you know we'll be there in a nanosecond to rescue his ass."

"Which he'll tell us he didn't need." She laughed.

"Exactly!"

They both laughed then, fondly remembering their friend's numerous close calls that he never acknowledged. "Remember that time,-"

"Remember the dragon lake-" They both laughed again as they both pictured times that they had gone to rescue Jarrandon when he 'didn't need anything'.

"Idiot," Arichel laughed fondly.

"So you're headed out right after breakfast?" asked Lath. At her nod he said, "I am too. I'm heading to various kingdoms to collect updates about the missing children and not share what we know." He grimaced. "I'm going to feel terrible about that in some places."

She laid a hand against his for a moment. "I know. Hopefully you won't need to lie outright. And maybe, try to focus on the planning for when we bring the children home rather than not sharing."

"Yeah." He took another sip of coffee. "What about you?"

"I'm going to go stir crazy waiting," she answered truthfully. "And I won't even be able to release the tension with a good battle workout."

"When I get back-" Lath started to offer.

"We'll see. Thank you," Arichel groaned inwardly. Practicing swords with Lath would take her mind off anything else and exhaust her. But she would be covered in bruises for a week and avoid all possible stairs for just as long. "I'm also meeting with someone to research earth mythology. They have some uncanny truths about this world in myths. Maybe they do about this other world, too."

Lath nodded, "Interesting. I hadn't thought of that." He finished his coffee with a loud slurp and his sandwich was gone too. "Right then, love. I'll see you in a couple days." He moved over behind her and gave Arichel a leanover hug. "He'll be fine. But if you want to talk about it and don't want to with your husband, sweet though he is, I'll chat anytime."

"Thanks." Arichel knew he absolutely meant it. She could call him anytime day or night and he would drop anything he could, just to let her vent her feelings. She knew that he knew she would do the same for him.

As soon as she was done eating, she changed into running clothes of shorts and a thin, long sleeved tee and Traveled to Earth. She didn't even bother going into her house, but started walking to the running trails. Kingdom Trails, they were called. It was time to let her brain run, too, and clear itself. The sun was shining, but the morning air was still cool. There wasn't a breeze, but the trails were mostly in the shade. Arichel began walking and then jogging. As she began, her mind was still stumbling into concrete walls, but as her strides lengthened, her thoughts began to untangle too.

Chapter 9 - Waiting

Arichel pounded up the last bit of the hill, her sneakers slapping the packed, dirt path in the woods. The break in the trees ahead was the dirt road, but from here that was the only clue that she wasn't deep in the woods. Not a sound joined her except the normal woods sounds of the leaves whispering on the branches and a squirrel chattering. Her loud breathing muffled the sounds of everything else. She was not in shape for a real run. Not even close. Imagine if she were in armor.

Her thoughts were a little clearer, though.

Once out on the road, she walked a little farther up the hill and then took another road to head back to her house. By the time she walked the quarter mile back to the hill, down, and then the flat, her breathing was normal and the muscles were stretched out again. She jogged a little more until she reached her steep driveway. Arichel paused to grab the mail out of the black metal mailbox and then walked up the steep, gravel driveway. Once inside, she splashed water on her red face and gulped down a glass of water. Then with a refilled glass, she sat at the kitchen table to go through the mail. She saw right away that most of it was junk.

Moving most of the junk out of her way, Arichel had two pieces of mail left. One was an electric bill, and she would leave the envelope on the table until she paid it with her phone. The other was more interesting. It was an invitation to tea at the Haskell Free Library.

More than likely this tea party was a fundraiser, but that didn't change the location. It was one of those unique places built by two different communities coming together to share resources and build a place to join as a community. What was more unique about this building was that it was built by Americans and Canadians and sat right on the international border. In fact, a red line was painted on the floor to mark the border. Once inside, you could freely cross the line as much as you needed, but outside you needed to be aware of which side of the border you were on. There were a few other rules too, like that food couldn't cross the line, interesting to see how they would handle the tea party. But what struck her, was that this library had a huge collection of folklore and mythology books. In fact, there was a complete room devoted to it, which she had forgotten about until just now.

She pulled out her cell, and pressed the screen for 'Kerri'. After two rings a thick brogue answered, "Top of the mornin' to ya lass, although we're almost to afternoon, here."

"G'mornin, MacKerrit. D'ya have a minute?"

"Aye, Lass. Anything for you."

"You're a flirt." She paused for him to stop laughing, and then asked,

"What are you doing tomorrow afternoon?"

"Hmm, let me look at the calendar. Hold on a minute." The phone went muffled like he was holding it against his hand, but in a moment he was back. "There's nothing I can't switch around. What do you need?"

"Hmm, not *need* so much need as *want*. Would you come to tea with me tomorrow at 2, instead of meeting on Wednesday?"

There was dead silence for a beat on the other end, and Arichel could just imagine MacKerrit's face as he tried to puzzle out her words and if there was a puzzle to her words, or what she really meant.

"It really is tea, MacKerrit," she added. "You want to ask me where or why."

"Uhhuh. Where?" he asked dutifully.

"Haskell Free Opera House and Library."

"Never heard of it."

"No," she paused and then continued, "you probably haven't. It's a cool building though, where it's built. Look it up. But what's important is that they're having a tea party and they have a phenomenal room of folklore and mythology."

"Ahh, I see." Another bit of muffled noise came over the line and then MacKerrit spoke again. "Aye lass, tea tomorrow it is. Shall I meet you there or elsewhere?"

"There is fine, but be mindful that with all the little side streets it's easy to cross the border several times unintentionally."

"Yep. Understood. See you tomorrow, then." MacKerrit disconnected with more of a goodbye than his normal.

Again now, Arichel was left alone with no real task, and a brain on overdrive.

This week was stress overdrive, first her dear friend, Kri to the dragons and now her lover, Jarrandon to this new world. Missing children, a plague, and a new world were just extra. It was much easier not to worry when she was the one in danger. So Arichel sorted and threw in a load of laundry and then unloaded the dishwasher. She had swept before they left, so that was fine.

Then, she grabbed her laptop and a cold drink and headed out to the backyard to sit in a lawn chair, bask in the sun, and work on Earth's puzzles. Kri had said, *"Arichel, they told me to tell you that the plague on earth is connected. You won't be able to cure the plague, but you can help some by showing them the Hedges."*

Without knowing more about the third world, puzzling the connection seemed futile, better to focus on the hedges.

Hedges are boundaries, living fences, generally. So is it the boundary, or the plants? Or, the magic associated with the hedgerows that I need to figure out? Arichel tapped her fingers on the edge of the laptop as she thought. *Traditionally hedgerows were the border between the kept, orderly spaces and the wild, so they were the boundary between mortals and magic. A portal between worlds...it's got to be that. It's got to be the thinning of the veil, the thinning between worlds at the hedges that allows the magic through. But if the Good magic can come through so can every other energy...How would I even test that?*

Wearing a crown is lonely business, but Arichel would pour her energies into this puzzle and hope to solve this mystery at least. It would be so much easier to be in a death duel like with Bryongan Le Bryon. Swing the sword, pivot, block, feint, swing, up on toes, crouch low, and dance on and on. Beyond the point of arms and hands being weights, then so tired they're numb, and the entire view narrowed to the ten feet around you, the only part of the battle that matters is what can be seen and felt next to you. Smells no longer exist, ears stopped ringing long before, and the focus narrowed to just the dance.

And then there was the prophecy, which was just as unhelpful.

Wearing a crown meant no freedom most of the time. A crown left few choices but those for the realm and in her case, realms. The only thing keeping the crown wearer sane was his or her court, their Inner Circle of trusted friends and allies.

Arichel took a breath and pushed her shoulders back, straightening the metaphorical crown. *Fuck this shit. There's a hedge on the path to the Fairy Glen trails, aptly named ironically. Time to explore.*

Setting her laptop down and plugging it in, she slipped her moonstone into her pocket, her emerald bracelet on her wrist, a vial of wolfsbane on a delicate chain around her neck, and a variety of daggers in her soft boots, under the hem of her shorts, and along her arms. Then she switched the tshirt she had been wearing for a flowing, dark shirt with long, loose sleeves that hid all the upper blades. Last, she popped a piece of mint gum in her mouth to settle some nerves and briskly walked out the door to walk down to the trails.

The Kingdom Trails were known for difficult trails named "Coronary Bypass" and literal names like "Cow Path" and finally silly, fun names like "Fairy Glen". Arichel had considered running down to the crossover trail to

Fairy Glen, and as soothing as a run might be, she wanted her little safety gems and blades as she had no idea what was about to happen, but they were not conducive to running, or even jogging. But, walking briskly still gave her a chance to feel the sun on her face, the wind teasing her hair, and the earth sending soothing energy into her soul. She needed to be grounded, she wasn't being completely stupid.

She laughed at herself as she walked. Well, yes, she was being a little stupid. She should have back-up for this since she actually had no idea what would happen when she started playing with energies at the hedgerow.

She sent out a mental message. Her first thought had been to send it to Jarrandon, but he wasn't back yet. Her heart wanted to hiccough at that, but she pushed it down. Adovey was available and so was Kri. Adovey and Kri were a force united, Adovey and she were a force united, and Kri and she had been friends and through battles enough times to know just how the other wielded their thoughts and their weapons. They could weigh the other's choice of risks and the opportunities without a second's breath as easily as their own. They were waiting when she arrived at the signpost for Fairy Glens.

"Couldn't you teleport?" asked Kri with a quirked eyebrow.

"I could have, but I wanted to charge."

Instantly Adovey's stance changed from casual to on guard. "Just what are we doing here?"

Kri looked at Arichel and chuckled deep in her throat. "We, my Love, are here to grab her and run, if needed. And our dear Arichel is going to experiment with magic."

Arichel laughed back, "Basically. I'm not really sure if this will work, and I'm not sure what "this" is that I'm trying to do…but it's the best I've got." As they walked into the shade of the trees, along the broad trail, she explained what she knew, and what she largely theorized.

"It's a sound theory," Adovey agreed, "but how do we test it?"

Kri just grinned and gave Arichel a *Good Luck* look.

"We don't. There's no test. I'm just going to call the magic through."

"What the *actual* fuck, do you mean?" He repeated himself, "What the actual fuck, do you mean?" Adovey's face was incredulous.

"I don't have a plan, I don't know what will happen, I don't even know what to hope to have happen so there is no test."

"Hence we're here, Love," reminded Kri. "If this goes south we grab her and teleport out."

Arichel slid her eyes to Kri and the understanding was met in her eyes. There was too much unknown, but there wasn't any way to learn except by trying it.

Kri and Adovey flanked Arichel, facing away but able to see her from the corner of their eyes. Warriors all of them, they felt the scene, they breathed the scene, they listened, and they looked. All three were hyperaware.

Arichel reached out her hands and felt a faint vibration as she almost touched the hedge, a living wall and apparently, a magical boundary too. Gently she pushed her hand in, and it was like sinking her hand into warm fudge. Immediately, the magic oozed a warm, soft, pliant, almost-liquid to surround her hand and move up her fingers towards her palm. She wiggled her finger softly and felt the magic swirl and eddy thickly.

Kri was watching her face intently in her peripheral. "What does it feel like?"

"Like warm caramel." Arichel smiled for a moment then bit her lips together as she reached further in to feel the other side. "It's clearly a wall of soft energy and I can easily move through this warm energy, but I'm not sure what else can. It's a few inches thick, I'm teasing through to see what's on the other side."

"You have magical fingers," smirked Adovey, "I'm sure you can tease this energy to new heights."

Kri and Arichel both snorted.

The air seemed to cool as she pushed her hand further in. Her fingers broke through the other side and it was very much cooler on the other side, like sticking one's fingers through a hole in a mitten into the snow.

Just on the other side, a light breeze moved and little threads of a different energy, strings of magic, tickled her fingers. Arichel pinched her fingers together as she tried to grasp one but the magical string danced and slipped like oiled silk. Finally, she pinched on and wrapped it quickly around her fingers and then looped it tighter around her middle finger, closing her fist with the other fingers folded over her middle finger, holding that thread tight.

She firmly but slowly pulled her hand back, but now the warm caramel was more like warm fudge, coalescing and thickening into a soft solid. Soon her hand was being squeezed and then as she pulled free of the physical hedge her hand nearly couldn't fit while fisted closed. She slid her left hand in, straight out like a blade, wedging in and then around her other hand. Using her left hand now, to hold the slippery thread of magic, she adjusted her grip in her dominant hand and Arichel steadily pulled.

"My Love?" Kri spoke softly to Adovey.

"Yeah, I see it."

"What's happening?" asked Arichel, but she didn't dare look, afraid to lose her tenuous grasp of the magic.

"I'm not sure," answered Adovey quietly.

"No, I can't tell either, but it seems like a flock of small, dark birds." Kri said in her serious, hushed voice. "But it's not a normal flock of birds, and it's coming straight at us."

"I've got the magic in my hand," Arichel said, "but the hedge isn't happy that I'm pulling it through. It's not warm and soft anymore, it's firming up. Can you hold them off as I pull this through?"

"Uhhuh," and "Yut," they grunted.

Arichel steadily pulled as one might pull in a heavy weighted bag on a chain from the bottom of the ocean. She felt as if she really were pulling it from that distance, too. Each time she could pull back enough for a quick regrip she would wrap the magic coil around her hand. Luckily it was unlike any real thread or rope. The magic itself was more malleable and was happy to wrap around her hand in wide bands. Eventually, she pushed those bands up her arm like you might push up the warm sleeves of a sweatshirt. Still she pulled, hard and strong as the hedge fought her to hold the magic back. Sweat trickled down her back and between her breasts. Her legs, strong enough for hours of battle, could feel the burn of locking and holding while she leaned back and pulled.

Beside her, she could feel and hear, and sometimes see a fight of swords against black feathers, talons, and beaks. Clearly not birds though, based upon the humanlike squawks and rancid smell.

It felt like hours, but was perhaps only minutes. Or maybe it was days. All that mattered was pulling the coils of magic through the tiny fissure in the hedge.

Pain lanced through her head, and with a gasp Arichel almost fell forward. She felt him gasp or maybe she heard it, the pain bubbling in his chest and the taste of fear in his throat.

"Help him!" she screamed. "Leave me, get Jarrandon!"

Adovey glanced at her, hearing the terror in her voice, and almost lost an eye to a savage dirty talon. "Yeah, we're not leaving you," he said.

"You have to, he's hurt!" Arichel's eyes stung with tears. She wouldn't let go of the magic until she was done, and she was entirely willing to sacrifice herself in the process to make it succeed. But Jarrandon was hurt, maybe dying!

"They're on the way," grunted Kri. "Lath and Captain."

"Good thinking!" Adovey grinned appreciatively to Kri, while batting an oily wing away from the back of her head.

"Thank you," grunted Arichel, her almost-full attention back on her game of tug o'war.

"We got you," said Kri simply. They had been through these situations enough times through the centuries - all of them, in every single role.

The ozone popped and Riv dropped in beside them, in a defensive stance and swinging her blades as soon as she could see. With Riv there to help defend against the harpy-like birds, Kri dropped back and helped Arichel steadily pull the magic through. The two of them were sweating as if they were in the constant bird battle, but soon the cord of living magic grew thinner, until suddenly the tail whipped through.

"Now what?!" shouted Kri to Arichel.

"Retreat somewhere in this world!" shouted Arichel back. "My house!" She no sooner decided this than she grabbed Riv's upper arm, and Kri grabbed Adovey and they translocated around and over the hill to the house.

They stood there a moment, the warriors leaning forward resting hands on knees and breathing hard. Arichel sagged down to the ground and cradled the living magic in her arms. They listened, but the birdlike creatures didn't follow.

Arichel slowly, and almost absently, stroked the magic, like soothing an animal cuddled in her arms. She sent out a questioning feel to Lath.

Immediately he sent back, *We've got him. We're in the house, and Captain has gone to get Doctor Hellenesprout. Are you three ok?*

Arichel let out a huge breath, "They've got him in the house. Dr Hellenesprout is on the way." To Lath, *Yeah, we're good now. Figuring out our next step. And Lath?*

Yeah?

Thank you!

Of course. He sent a fluttering touch, the equivalent of a hug with mindspeak.

"Ok, oh wise one. Now what the fuck are you going to do with that energy you're holding?" Adovey's sarcasm gave his voice a harsh edge.

"I don't know yet," Arichel admitted, "But the dragons said the cure was with the hedges."

"Well that bloody clears it all up." Adovey wiped his face, but a tiny black feather still curled against his ear. "I need a beer."

"Hell yeah!" agreed Riv.

"Agreed."

Adovey stepped into the house and came right back out holding four cans of beer and one bottle. He handed a can each to Riv and Kri, and then the bottle to Arichel. He drained one can and then popped a second.

"Ok," started Adovey again, a little calmer now, though the feather kept tickling his ear. "So, the dragons said the hedges were key so you decided to tease the magic out of the magical boundary between two worlds?"

"Umm, I see where you're coming from, but not quite." Arichel took a deep drink of her beer, and then rested the cold bottle against her forehead. "There is still magic in the hedge, so the boundary still seems solid. I-we pulled this ball of magic from the other side of the hedge, and the hedge

resealed itself just as soon as she popped through."

"Uhhuh-" Adovey prodded, but was interrupted by Kri.

"He has a valid point you know," Kri was brusque but not unkind. "We do need to figure out what you do with your new pet, and the dragons' advice is rather...vague."

"Yeah." Arichel continued to stroke the magic like a pet and in exchange it wrapped itself up and around her arm and rested against her shoulder.

Apparently, it was a rather cute little thing.

Chapter 10 - A little Pet

"You have to admit the dragons' advice is a little vague," stated Kri.

"No, you're right," agreed Arichel. "And, I just want to get back to the house and check on Jarrandon-"

"Doctor Hellenesprout is the best," interrupted Adovey.

"I know. But I want to figure this out now." Arichel drank the last of her beer and set the bottle by her feet. She had slipped out of her shoes and her toes were digging into the grass. "Somehow this little pet here is the cure to this plague, but I don't know how. She can't possibly be led around to touch every infected person. So how does she cure the world?" *Fuck!* Arichel dropped her head backwards and stretched her neck side to side to stretch out some of the tension.

The ozone popped again, and MacKerrit dropped in. His face was ashen except for dark circles under his eyes. "Thank Goddess you're here, Lass," Mackerrit groaned, looking at Arichel. "I quite feel like shite, suddenly."

"You look like shit, MacKerrit," said Riv bluntly.

"Aye, lass." MacKerrit closed his eyes. Arichel moved over to him and laid her hand against his forehead. As she did, a wisp of the magic slipped down and touched his bare arm.

Mackerrit jumped up and howled in pain.

"What the fook was that? Something bit me or stung me!"

Arichel blinked fast, Kri bit her lip in thought.

"What are you talking about?" asked Adovey.

MacKerrit was swatting at his arms and legs as if to brush some pest away.

Arichel looked at Kri and raised an eyebrow. Kri nodded back, "Try it."

"MacKerrit, do you trust me?" asked Arichel.

"Do ye see it? What bit me?" asked MacKerrit, still brushing off his clothes. "'Course I do, Lass."

"Look at me, then," Arichel waited til he made eye contact. "I don't think you were bit exactly. MacKerrit, do you have the virus?"

"Ohhhh," Riv exhaled quietly.

MacKerrit's eyes narrowed. "Aye, Lass, that's what I came to ask ye for help with."

"I think it was this magic that...stung you, but I think it will cure you, too. At least that's the riddle we think the dragons gave us."

MacKerrit laughed bitterly, "Dragon's advice. Now that will clear it all up." He closed his eyes for a moment, as if completely exhausted. "Do it, Lass, whatever it is ye want to try. That is why I've come, after all."

As if it understood, the pet of magic slid a tendril down Arichel's arm and around her finger like fine filigree. Arichel reached her finger towards MacKerrit with her brow furrowed. Just as her fingertip brushed his arm, the tendril thinned some more and kissed his skin. MacKerrist hissed but didn't move. The magic thinned and spread until it was no more than a ghost of fog over his arm. Then it pulled back. As the magic withdrew, Arichel leaned back also.

They stared at MacKerrit.

"Well," he paused like he was evaluating every molecule of his body. "That wasna terrible, but I could be convinced to not do it again."

"How do you feel?" asked Riv.

"Well, I'm not sure this magic is me favorite, but I'll live." MacKerrit pursed his lips and gave a quick nod. "Actually, I think I feel better like I might actually live. Don't get me wrong, I am still exhausted, but I don't think I have the headache any more, Lass, nor am I so ...odd feeling."

"Your color is better," commented Adovey.

The magic had curled back up and coiled in on itself to be like a warm stole around Arichel's shoulders, nestled under her ear. She reached up her hand and stroked it with her finger like she would under a cat's chin. A wisp stretched forward, over her fingers.

"Look at that," Riv said watching, "if I didn't know better I would say that magic has the spirit of a cat in it. It really is a pet."

"A pretty astounding pet," added Arichel. "I can't hear anything, but I swear it feels like it is purring, just like a cat would."

Kri had been observing and not saying anything yet. Now she spoke softly, "Like a cat or like a dragon?" All eyes snapped to her.

"Hmm," pondered Arichel. "Maybe."

Kri continued, "Ok Pet, I'm not sure what to call you,"

The wisp of magic bobbed forward a little. "You seem quite sentient. I think you have awareness, and I think you can help us, if we know what to ask for."

"Look," breathed Adovey.

The magic was not only moving slightly further onto the left side of Arichel's body, closer to Kri, but it was slightly glowing now with faint swirls of pink and purple iridescence.

"I think that's a 'yes,'" said Riv with a smile.

"You can help us, can't you, Little One?" asked Arichel.

The magic glowed brighter in response to Arichel's question and pearlescent light swirled through it, like an affirmative.

"Great," said Adovey, "Now, we just need to figure out how to communicate with a color shifting, swirl of magic. We wouldn't want a dragon's task to be too easy, now."

Kri snorted a laugh, "Right."

"At least she understands us." Arichel rubbed her temples.

"True," agreed Riv with a smile.

Kri stood up, "C'mon MacKerrit, let's bring you to the house. I would like Dr Hellenesprout to double check our theory. You still look a little loosekneed, I'll pop us over." Kri reached down a hand and grabbed MacKerrit.

"Take a raincheck on a visit to that library, Lass?" his brogue was stronger.

Arichel smiled, "Of course."

Kri shifted her hand to his elbow, and she and MacKerrit disappeared.

"Now what?" asked Adovey.

"No fucking clue," Arichel rubbed her temple again. "We can't bring her around to every single person, not that they would all be willing anyway."

"Nope. That sounds like a great way to get shot, quite honestly."

"You're not kidding," laughed Adovey.

Arichel shaded her eyes to look at Adovey standing so the sun was bright behind him. There was an idea tugging at her brain, but she just couldn't quite grasp it. "I don't dare try to travel with her, but I really want to go back."

Adovey came over and pulled her head against his chest. "I know. I can't imagine how hard it is for you to be away from him. We've got the best taking care of him though."

"Yeah."

Riv reached over and squeezed her leg, "We'll figure this out. We always do." She hopped up, "Time for more beer." She moved into the house to "reload".

Adovey rubbed Arichel's head in commiseration and then shifted his hand down to massage her neck. The little magic reached up and tickled his hand. "Stop that," he laughed. "Cute little bugger isn't it?"

"You know," pondered Arichel out loud. "We keep thinking of this as a cute little kitten-like pet, but this magic is older than all of us. Probably older than the earth even."

Riv returned and handed out the beer, "Yeah, maybe older than the universe."

The magic almost seemed to giggle and then curled up and rolled about, up and down Arichel's arms.

"Spry though," snorted Riv.

A few hours and a fair amount of alcohol and sunshine later, the idea that had been dancing just out of reach, finally blossomed.

"Alright, Pet," began Arichel, they had settled on this name being as good as any and Pet didn't seem to mind. "You can clearly move through space, and maybe time, I dunno, but you're not tied to a specific spot, right? It was the hedge that was holding you, or something else pulling you back, as I was pulling you through?"

Pet had somehow shifted towards Arichel as she spoke, and glowed in warm tones - an affirmative.

Arichel nodded, "Uhhuh, and so you can go wherever you choose?"

Pet slowly sank a little, and the internal glow dimmed a little.

"You can't go anywhere you want?" The glow brightened some, and flickered, but Pet rose back up.

"That's the best *maybe* I've seen from a non-talking, shapeless entity yet," laughed Adovey.

Pet flicked a thread out and caressed his cheek, then flicked him.

"I think she's flirting with me." They all laughed. Even Pet, who shifted sunshine yellow and bounced around for a moment.

Arichel was thinking out loud again, but conversationally, Pet did her best to answer. "You can't go anywhere, but you can move about."

Pet glowed a warm pink.

"Is there something in particular that controls you or a universal sorta law?"

Pet shifted and turned into a waterfall of smoke.

"Yeah, that was poorly worded on my part." Arichel grimaced and tried again, this time pausing for the color shift, "Are you controlled by another?...or following laws of magic?"

Pet responded favorably to the latter question.

"Mmmhmm. So, that should be pretty easy to work within. We can't eliminate the virus, or it leaves a vacuum, but we can cure it."

Pet coiled up and sat on Arichel's shoulder like a snake, a cute little cobra. She seemed to go to sleep then.

The hours passed, Arichel growing more agitated wanting to be with Jarrandon, but remaining focussed to the task at hand. As dusk started to fall, they switched their focus to whether the magic could travel with Arichel to Aegnya, or whether she would be willing to stay with someone else.

As the sky darkened, Pet stirred. She lifted her head looking up into the sky, waiting for something.

"Good morning again, Little Pet," crooned Arichel. "Did you have a good nap?"

Pet ducked and rubbed under Arichel's chin. Then, she returned her attention to the night sky.

"What is she doing?" asked Adovey. They all watched Pet, they could see the mist was tensely expectant.

Suddenly, a shooting star, ridiculously bright, burned across the sky. Pet danced around animatedly, almost dripping excitement.

"You like shooting stars?" asked Arichel.

Pet undulated and danced, but didn't glow with the affirmative pink colors from earlier.

"You like stars, not just shooting stars?" probed Riv.

Now, Pet began to glow her warm, pink light.

"That makes sense," murmured Arichel, "She looks like starlight."

Pet whirled and danced at that. She jumped up above their heads and coalesced into beams of light and then shattered into millions of flecks of mist and light, like tiny, stars twinkling above their heads. She fell upon them like a light mist, pulling together and reconvening on Arichel's shoulders. She rubbed up against Arichel's face, if she made any noise, she would have been purring. Arichel chewed on her bottom lip.

"You don't just like stars, but you are a star?" asked Arichel.

Pet glowed brighter. "So why are you down here, not up in the light up there?"

Pet danced around and spun, but couldn't answer this question. Her glow brightened some, and flickered, before Pet curled back up.

"She has mastered the 'maybe,'" laughed Adovey.

Pet shot a blip of light at him that stopped above his head and then showered down like fireworks.

"Are other stars like you?" asked Arichel, following the thread of an idea.

Pet flickered, but didn't change her light levels.

"Hmm, I mean, can other stars form like you, and heal like you?"

Pet brightened a little at this with a warm tangerine color.

"And, can you rise back up to join the other stars?"

Pet pulsed brighter.

"If you do that, can you come back down here, if you wanted to?" Pet glowed pink.

"What are you thinking?" asked Adovey.

Arichel chewed her bottom lip a moment more, "Well, I'm thinking out loud, but see if this makes sense. I think Pet here is a star, or *is* starlight, or something like that." Pet pulsed. "We also saw that she can heal this plague." Pet pulsed again, slowly. "So if she is like the other stars, and if they are like her, it seems that starlight is somehow the cure for the plague."

"Ohh," breathed Riv.

"Now, where I'm stumbling is whether we can have Pet here gather her friends and whether the starlight can fall on every person and heal them, and then whether she can return to hanging out as she pleases."

Pet pulsed slowly but glowed.

"I think that's Star for 'probably,'" grinned Adovey.

"Is *probably* good enough?" asked Arichel.

Pet flickered her lights and then rose above them dusting them all with dots of light. These light dots were warm but not hot and felt like they sizzled into the skin.

"I think we were just inoculated with stardust," laughed Riv.

Pet flicked her tail, then she roped herself around Arichel enveloping her in misty warmth. She flicked Arichel's nose and then shot up in the sky and was almost immediately out of sight.

"Ummm..." Adovey started.

"Yeah. Did we just save the world or waste the day?" asked Riv with a laugh.

"I dunno, but I'm going to see Jarrandon." Arichel stood and teleported as soon as the words left her mouth. She landed in the Traveling Square and immediately turned to rush up to the house. Lath opened the heavy front door as she arrived and folded her into an embrace.

Chapter 11 - Reunited

"It's all right," Lath soothed into Arichel's hair. He's mostly slept, but he knows why you couldn't be here earlier."

"Is he-"

"He'll be alright. Dr Hellensprout left, you know she wouldn't have done that if she were gravely concerned."

Arichel let out a breath that she didn't know she had been holding. Her shoulders loosened a little.

"Go see him, but take a moment to wash your face and gather yourself. He was sleeping as I felt you arrive." Lath hugged her and then gave her a little push towards the tiny bathroom off the entry hall.

"Thanks, Lath," said Arichel with a soft smile.

"Course," Lath smiled back. I'll send some food up for you both too. I guarantee you're gonna wake him up.

She snickered along with his knowing laugh. "Thanks," she grinned back at him.

Arichel did take a moment to compose herself and then lightly ran up the stairs two at a time to Jarrandon's bedroom. She quietly eased open the door, but she needn't have bothered.

"Good, come here," Jarrandon's voice was a little horse, but sounded hale enough. "Get your perfect, little ass on this bed beside me."

Arichel laughed, and jumped up on the bed, "Not so little, y'know."

"Perfect though," Jarrandon pulled her down beside him and wrapped her under his arm. Arichel laid her face, tentatively against the rough cotton bandage on his otherwise naked chest. "It's fine, it doesn't hurt." Arichel raised an eyebrow he couldn't see. "Well, not much. It's a little tender." He acknowledged. "No, you don't!" he scolded as she made to move off him. "This is what I need."

Arichel snuggled back down and his arm snaked around her and cupped one breast. Almost immediately though, Lath knocked at the door and after pausing a very long moment, he pushed open the door.

"This is your fair warning," Lath growled, "You had better cover yourselves. I've seen you both naked, and I don't want to do it again, especially imagining some of the positions you could be entangled in."

Arichel thought about throwing a tasseled pillow at him, but decided not to because he was carrying food. She pushed up and off the bed to help Lath with the steaming plates. House materialized wooden trays on the bed and the three of them settled in to eat.

Shortly after their first bites, another knock and giggles came at the door and Kri, Riv, and Adovey pushed in carrying in their dishes. Heavy furniture was shoved aside, ceramic bowls balanced and everyone settled in to shovel food in their mouths. It had been a long day on top of overlong weeks.

Adovey held up his glass of foamy beer, "Cheers, Brother, welcome home!"

"Cheers!" the others echoed.

"Welcome home," echoed Arichel.

"Hafta say, I'm glad to be back," grinned Jarrandon. "It was a good trip... right up until the end."

"Eat first, while it's hot," ordered Kri. "We all have plenty to share, but

Jarrandon needs to build his strength back up."

Arichel snorted, "It sounds like we're all hungry, but yeah." Indeed the slurping and gulping happening in the room was all about satiating hunger and had nothing to do with manners.

Soon enough silver stopped scraping pottery and they were all sitting back with a sigh, holding or swirling a glass.

"Alright Boyo," said Arichel with a smile, "Spill it. What the hell happened?"

"I heard you had a little mischief of your own?"

"Nahuh, you first," Arichel replied with mock seriousness.

"Yes, M'Lady." Jarrandon was grinning as he spoke, but then his face grew grave as he swirled his whiskey and swallowed it down.

"Yeah, so," he paused for a moment gathering his thoughts. "There are a lot of pieces and they are so tangled, it's hard to lay it out to you in any real order. Just bear with me." Seeing his friends giving him rapt attention and waiting, Jarrandon continued. "So I didn't get to gather as much information as I wanted to. Luckily, there wasn't much of a language barrier. I didn't talk much and pretended I had a stutter to cover my accent."

"Smart," grunted Adovey.

"Thanks."

Adovey lifted his glass, but didn't say anything else so Jarrandon could continue.

"Yeah. So, a quiet stutterer is accepted in most places so I could sit and listen. Pretty quickly I learned that the children are being used. Easy now Riv, the kids are being used in a task that only children can do. So they're valuable. And therefore they are treated alright."

"Taking them from their homes is *not* alright!" growled Riv.

"No, but it's not as bad as it could be. They aren't being sacrificed, or sold for sex. I had prepared my heart for both of those scenarios. Or, something worse."

"Worse?" breathed Riv. "What could be worse?"

"There's worse, Love. But hush, it's not what's happening now, so let's not fret." Lath leaned over and squeezed Riv's thigh. She looked at him with huge eyes filled with tears, but she nodded and sat back quietly.

"So these children are being used to mine a particular essence that only children can touch, some say only innocent children, but it seems to be any able children. Because they need healthy children, the children are being decently housed in dormitories, clothed, and fed. What they don't have, aside from their families, is a children's life. There doesn't seem to be any education or playtime, just working and sleeping. It seems to depend on the mine whether they have a day off and whether they can celebrate their religions."

"So, some mine owners are better than others?" asked Lath in a steely quiet voice.

"Yeah." Jarrandon bit his lip, hearing the full implication in the question. "Some are better but none seem terrible aside from the whole kidnapping and forced labor." He gave Riv a sympathetic smile, then continued, "So I was able to get a pretty good look at one of the camps, it actually looks like a small town built near a mine. Then, I was able to find another of these camps. That's where I ran into a little trouble."

"Yes," said Adovey, pouring a refill for Jarrandon, "tell us about this little trouble you found."

"Yeah," laughed Jarrandon softly, "so I found the second camp and shortly after, it found me. The dormitories were pretty much the same, the kids looked ok, fed and healthy at least. I tried to get a little closer to the mine to see just what it is that only children can touch. Apparently, that's a secret that they didn't want to share. The camps may not be well guarded but the mines are. I felt the ward when I tripped it, but it was too late. They had an immediate response and they overwhelmed us a little. We lost one man-"

"Who?" barked Captain.

"Michaels."

"Good man. If they didn't surprise you, they must be excellent fighters."

"He was, and yes, they're good. A few of us took some hits, but they suffered more." A harsh gleam entered Jarrandon's eyes for a minute. The pain of losing a team member had probably made him fight like a berserker. "We got away, but only barely. We won't surprise them again."

"No," Arichel chewed inside her lip, "we won't. So if we can't surprise them, we'll make sure they know us very, very well." Arichel was just as much a warrior when a member of her team was hurt. Jarrandon's team was her team by extension, although his injuries alone would have brought out her deep fae instincts.

"So what do we do?" she looked around the room, "Do we move through "appropriate" channels and send a delegation or do we move straight to assault and rescue?"

Kri hadn't said anything until now, only sipping her wine and giving her rapt attention to Jarrandon. "I think, both simultaneously, is the best route."

Captain agreed, "Aye, distract and achieve."

"None of us are going to be very diplomatic, while the rest are in a rescue assault," argued Arichel.

"That's why Lath earns the big money," laughed Adovey.

"Hmph, is that so?" aske Lath. "Could you maybe make sure my bank account knows that?"

"Hmph."

"Yeah, good luck with that!"

Planning and arguing went late in the night. Even as they planned, each of them knew it was only a slight chance that any of their plans or back up plans, would actually go as expected. In situations like this, their centuries together meant that they knew how the others thought, knew the cadence of their breathing, inherently knew their strengths and their impulses. The unknowns were the people of this new world. Luckily, the terrains were similar to what they knew.

"Til tomorrow then, when we make a peaceful encounter whilst stealing back our children." Kri summed it up well as she said goodnight and glided from the room.

Everyone had left Jarrandon's bedroom following their planning session, except Arichel and Adovey. Jarrandon of course had remained in his bed in his own room, too.

"Want me to leave?" asked Adovey.

Arichel looked at Jarrandon, clearly leaving it up to him.

"Nah, stay. Not sure how much moving I can do right now." He chuckled deep in his throat. "I'm stiff but not in any good way." "We can fix that," Arichel said with a wicked smile and climbed back on the bed, lithely sliding up his body. Adovey just leaned back and watched.

House dimmed the lights, warmed the air a touch, and locked the doors. Arichel moved to the side and pushed the blankets aside. She paused a moment looking at the new cuts and scrapes, bruises crisscrossing old scars. She ran her fingers over the bruises on his thighs. Goosebumps jumped up across Jarrandon's skin. Her lips followed her fingers, her tongue dancing along, up his thighs and along his ribs. His hand came down and softly rested on her head, guiding her lower. She smiled and licked and teased the tip of his cock. He twitched in response and groaned.

Adovey dropped his clothes and began stroking himself in time to Arichel as she sucked and licked. Jarrandon's cock grew each time it grazed the back of her throat until she held her breath and held him there a moment. Adovey came over and climbed on the bed beside them with Arichel between them. Arichel kept her hand on Jarrandon, stroking his cock. Then, she moved her mouth to Adovey's cock and teased him before swallowing him deep into her throat as he moaned.

Having achieved getting both of them hard and ready, Arichel climbed onto Jarrandon. His eyes snapped open as this wasn't her normal choice.

"Hey, you don't have to-" he started to say, but stopped when she shook her head.

"No, it's ok, let's try this, at least to start." She took his cock in her hand, stroking it a couple times first and then guided it inside her, slowly sinking down and enveloping him in her soft heat.

"Oh Gods," breathed Jarrandon, "You feel, that feels, ohhhh."

Arichel just laughed softly. She leaned forward, putting her hands on his chest, her weight on his shoulders. She slowly slid up and down, and after a few strokes, Jarrandon reached up using his hands against her waist, guiding her tempo and lifting some of her weight.

Adovey moved behind, straddling Jarrandon's legs, pressing up against Arichel's ass. He reached around, cupping her breasts, rubbing his thumbs against her nipples, and running his lips and then his teeth along her neck. Arichel shivered and softly laughed.

Jarrandon caught Adovey's eyes over Arichel's shoulder.

"Yeah?" Adovey lifted an eyebrow with the question.

"Yeah," Jarrandon then focuses on Arichel, "Baby, do you want us both?"

"Obviously," Arichel laughed. "But what do you mean? Both of you right now?"

"Yeah, if you want to."

"But only if you want to, Love," Adovey nibbled on her ear, and she could feel how much he wanted it.

"Yeah." Arichel twisted so she could reach her arms around Adovey and kissed deeply. After a moment, Jarrandon started moving inside her again, shifting her weight from her thighs against him, to posting on her knees again, Arichel rode him for a moment.

Then, Adovey broke the kiss and gently pushed Arichel down and forward against Jarrandons chest. Jarrandon lifted his head up and met her in a kiss. His strong arms enveloped her, as their kiss broke so he could watch Adovey.

Arichel lifted her hips a little to make it easier. Adovey positioned himself and then slowly pushed in. Almost in unison, Jarrandon and Adovey groaned in pleasure.

"You ok?" asked Adovey.

"Yeah," breathed Arichel. She lifted her weight up off Jarrandon's chest a little, acutely aware of the rough cotton bandages. He gripped her upper arms, offering stability that way. She turned her head to look back at Adovey who grinned in return.

"That's so tight," Adovey groaned.

"It feels soooo good," agreed Jarandon.

Arichel laughed again. This was one of those perfect moments, entwined with both her loves and so happy.

Adovey began pumping then, Arichel just closed her eyes and hung on for the ride. Really she didn't need to do anything and was afraid of disrupting the rhythm. After a moment Jarrandon began moving, too.

It took less than a minute before Arichel felt Adovey pull back and hover a moment before thrusting and holding deep. Jarrandon thrust twice more, then threw his head back and exploded into her depths as well. Arichel kissed the beating vein in Jarandon's neck, and then twisted and met Adovey's lips as they crashed into her own.

"Fucking amazing!" Adovey spoke against her lips, and then pulled back and said, "You are fucking amazing."

"Fuck, yes," agreed Jarrandon, "but it's hardly fair. I miss the next part."

"What do you mean?" asked Arichel as she and Adovey rolled off.

"C'mon, Baby," grinned Jarandon. "We both know you're going into a hot tub next, and the second part will happen there because you need to get off, too."

"You can't get wet?" asked Adovey.

"Nah, Dr Hellensprout said no extreme heat, and no tubs until these heal over a bit more."

"Well, shit," said Arichel.

"You can watch," offered Adovey.

Arichel bit her lip and lay completely still.

"No, go use my tub, but she doesn't like an audience."

Arichel let out a breath in a soft woosh. House began filling the tub with steamy water. She traced her nail along Jarrandon's ribs and then playfully kissed the tip of his cock as she rolled away.

"You're a brat!" Jarrandon called after her.

"That ass, though," murmured Adovey.

"All yours, right now."

"On my way, Baby!" called out Adovey as he rolled from the bed. "Sorry man."

Jarrandon settled for imagining the scene, as he heard Arichel's throaty giggle as Adovey slipped into the hot water beside her. He knew her groan of pleasure was probably from her neck being massaged and not anything sexual, but he grew hard just the same. Jarrandon pulled and stroked himself as he listened, then a burst of feeling slammed into his head. His whoosh of air matched Arichel's laughter and splash as he felt and heard Adovey lift her up and onto the edge of the tub.

It was a big walk-in style tub, like a hot tub on earth, with marble surrounding it, but House kept the stone nice and warm. Arichel's feet were in the hot water, her ass on the warm stones, her weight supported on her hands leaning behind her. Adovey pushed apart her knees, and she melted a little as he massaged her thighs, his thumbs moving closer and closer to her inner core. She closed her eyes and breathed deeply. He knelt down in front of her, the hot water up to his chest, foaming a little at the curry hair. Arichel shivered a little at the feel of his lips and then his beard against her inner thighs. His thumbs gently spread her already swollen lips, and his hot breath teased her clit.

Jarandon had never experienced sex quite like this. It was a little mind blowing and incredibly hot. He stroked his cock, eyes closed, feeling everything she felt and listening to their rustling and splashing in the other room.

Adovey licked her clit, never stopping and never moving off of it, but varying the speed and pressure. Arichel focused on the sensations and slowly shut her mind down of all the other thoughts buzzing through it. He could see her getting close as the muscles in her belly tightened. He gently ran a finger around and then gently between her swollen lips and drenched pussy. She lifted her ass ever so slightly, and he focused more pressure with his tongue. Her belly tightened more and he slid his finger down lower to her even-more sensitive skin. Then, she exploded. As she came, so did Jarandon again. Adovey used both hands to grip her thighs and he kept licking as her leg and belly muscles clenched and unclenched.

"Sweet mother!" Arichel gasped as she scooted back a little.

Adovey grinned as he wiped his face. "Did I get both of you?"

"Holy fuck!" was all Jarandon could manage.

Arichel dropped back into the hot water and let the heat soak into all her tired muscles. Adovey grabbed a towel and walked back into the bedroom to talk with Jarandon. She heard the door open and close softly as Adovey left. She considered in which bed and with whom she wanted to sleep with as she lounged soaking up the heat. It seemed unfair to have to choose, but the three of them never slept well in one bed. She should have asked House to bring in another bed.

Chapter 12 - Hide and Seek

"This is like a giant game of hide and seek," laughed Captain

"Or, Capture the Flag," agreed Adovey. "They must know we're coming for the kids."

"Yeah," said Captain, "but distracting them with a giant entourage at their royal headquarters had better give us an edge."

"The rest of the monarchs seem to think it's worth trying," said Jarrandon.

"At least everyone is joining in. But it's gonna get bloody."

"-Er," added Arichel.

"What?" asked Jarrandon while Captain chuckled.

"-Er. You're going to get bloodier," said Arichel.

"Yeah," agreed Adovey. He leaned over and kissed her then, another one of those deep kisses embedded with hundreds of years of love.

"Ready?" He asked the group.

"Let's do this," answered Captain, and Lath nodded.

Lath and Arichel went first, along with King and Queen Dafang, King Bryongan Le Bryon, King and Queen Tinkerrtin, and King McLaughlin.

Then, those lucky enough to be warriors today rather than diplomats, went through the same gate, but to different destinations. They had memorized the maps that Jarrandon had drawn, with the intention of leaving him home to recuperate. That rather loud discussion had ended when he quietly said, "I either travel with you, or on my own, but I will bring those children home."

Earlier today, they had agreed that each court would be assigned to a different mine and holding camp that Jarrandon had found, rather than mixing their armies and trying new communication strategies. Once there, they would open smaller, and temporary gateways to bring forth an their own army of rescuers.

If everything went as planned, and they knew it wouldn't, then the royal party of monarchs and ambassadors would distract the rulers of the new world, while the rest of Arichel's family would rescue all the children and bring them back, first to camps of first aid, hot showers, clothes, and fresh meals. Then to emergency counseling if needed. And shortly after to reunite with their families. They had no idea how long the children's recovery would be, but getting them back to the right world was the paramount concern. Riv was ready to battle until her hands fell off and then love and hug the children with her bloody stumps, if it wouldn't be too traumatizing. Arichel had all she could do to be on the royal distraction team rather than the battle team.

The Gate fairly hummed, and the wards rang incessantly as they traveled out. The hope was that they would be spread out enough to not be noticed, but if they were, that the New World would believe that they were making a domestic call, monarchs to monarchs, and just sending out preliminary guards for their own safety. It was somewhat reasonable, until the armies arrived, but hopefully they were deep in their meetings and ceremony then.

Arichel and Queen Eleynia Dafang had both worn stunning gowns, with plenty of jewels draped over themselves, and not a few weapons hidden underneath. They both wore ornate crowns with their hair curled and held high, also hiding numerous weapons. The kings and ambassadors, including Lath, wore ridiculously ornate swords that would have difficulty cutting bread, let alone being helpful in a battle. Or so it seemed, but truly the gem encrusted blades were but another sheath that could be easily released. They all hoped their magic was fully charged.

Just before Arichel was ready to step up to the gate, there was a *pop* of air and a very old, leather bound book appeared on the ground by her feet.

"What the?!" exclaimed Kri.

"No worries, Lass," soothed Lath, "It's just a last minute delivery for Arichel."

The title was embossed and painted with some sort of silver leaf, "Lost Land".

"Interesting," Arichel murmured.

"Do you think it's related to this?" asked Queen Eleynia Dafang.

"Pretty strong coincidence to not be, don't you think?" asked King Bryongan.

"Well, yeah."

Arichel opened up the book and groaned a little. The script inside was tiny, and faded black to brown in some places. Almost immediately though she could read that it was indeed about this new world. "Thank you," she murmured, pushing the feeling towards House. She didn't know for sure it was House that had apparated it to her at the last moment, but it seemed pretty likely, since everyone else 'on the case' was standing beside her. Everyone except MacKerrit, but even so, House would have had to let him send it through the wards, so regardless House deserved a thanks.

Kri came and looked over Arichel's shoulder and blew out a huff of breath. "Let's be starting with the table of contents and see what might help us most. Too bad we didn't have this last night to study."

Arichel hurriedly paged forward until they came to a page of headings. They both pointed simultaneously to "The Royal Houses and Court Life".

"We'll study this on the way, ok?"

"We'll have to, or our wayward armies will have problems, but let's send out a message, just the same, that we just received new intel and are delaying a few minutes. That will hold their impatience a touch," added Captain.

So Lath primed the gate for their location and held an arm of each of his ladies as they pored over the book. It wouldn't do for their lack of focus to land them in the middle of an ocean somewhere. The other monarchs followed through the gate in his wake.

Stepping through the gate, they were met with a cacophony of crashes and screams that startled the toughest among them. Heat and humidity slapped them in the face and slammed them in the chest.

"Shit, I forgot he said jungle," swore Arichel. "I was just thinking of vines and venomous critters, not heat and jungle animals. Are those frickin' birds that are making that racket?"

As if in answer, a particularly loud scream sounded and a rush of wings lifted off beside them.

"Damn," King Daviraf understated dryly.

"Yeah, ok, so the chapter on geographical features probably would have warned us, but oh well," said Lath dryly.

"Yeah," Arichel chuckled without humor and looked back at the book. "So, the *Losunkians*, as the people here are called, prefer ornate and large court appearances. Looking important pretty much equals being important. Apparently, we made a good guess. So far so good for Jarrandon."

"He is quite good at his job," added Lath quietly.

"He'd be better if he didn't get hurt," grumbled Arichel. "Anyway, large and formal is what the Losunkians seem to prefer. Also, they speak a tongue very similar to our language, which we also already knew. This makes sense as they both seem to come from the same root language. So, we may sound funny to them and vice versa, but we shouldn't have grammatical misunderstandings. Hopefully no unintentional wars due to language misunderstandings."

"No unintentional wars," snorted Lath.

"Hush," said Kri as she quickly elbowed him.

Arichel continued, ignoring Lath, "They have a hereditary government and it seems like it is more bloodline based and with many feuds disrupting the bloodlines."

"She means that they are cunts, and never have a ruling family for more than three generations and sometimes only one." Kri could read just as quickly as Arichel.

"One what?"

"One generation."

"Oh!" Defang laughed nervously. "Not so stable, huh?"

"Nope, so it won't be surprising if they expect that we are here to attack them and stage a coup. Keep your weapons handy," advised Lath.

"Oh, thank you for that venerable advice, oh wise one. Think we should sharpen them, too?" asked Bryongan dryly.

"Yeah. A little obvious. Sorry."

"A little," Bryongan agreed, "We have done this sort of thing before."

"A few times," Lath agreed with a tight smile.

Arichel paged through the book hurriedly, but didn't see anything else noteworthy to help them at the last minute. "Ok then. Anyone else feel Jarrandon's marker of where we should jump to?"

Bryongan nodded and held out his hands. Lath grunted an affirmative and linked arms with more of the party. Shortly, everyone was touching someone who could feel the marker and was ready to transport them.

"On your mark then," ordered Bryongan, "backs in, weapons ready, but not threatening, and smile! Ready?" Seeing everyone dip their heads in assent he counted down. "3...2...1...go!"

Simultaneously then, they all blurred out of sight and reappeared on a flagstone path, in front of a tall stone arched gate, opening out to a lake with a mountain behind it. It was a gorgeous view of the snow capped mountain.

"Psst," hissed Lath and their party spun around and shifted with ease. King Tinkerton and King Bryongan shifted to watch their rear. Queens Arichel, Tinkerton, Eleynia and Kri melted to the middle, and the other men flanked the ladies. Their party knew the queens weren't any less dangerous than the men, but sometimes deceiving appearances was worth more than the truth.

Four, thickset, scowling men were facing them. Each man held a drawn sword and a spear. A gong was ringing somewhere behind the men, and bells began to ring too. Not a joyful ringing, but a somber, warning, tolling.

"Hide and seek, remember," murmured Arichel.

Almost imperceptible nods met her, and telepathically, "Yeah, hold and delay. We know."

Soon eight more men ran up, only slightly winded, also brandishing spears and very sharp looking swords.

Arichel's throat was tight as if she were about to cry. She knew this feeling. She had felt it hundreds of times before. The fear that she had made a mistake. She wasn't afraid of her mistake hurting her, she had chosen this path, she had chosen the risk. No, she was afraid for her family, these friends that were more dear than family. She was afraid that she had made a mistake and led them into danger that was worse than they had prepared for. She was afraid that if something did happen to her, that the rest of her family: Jarrandon, Captain, and everyone currently rescuing the children, would then put themselves in risk again to rescue this part of the family.

That they would put themselves in danger to rescue *her*.

Arichel swallowed, and swallowed again as she reinforced her mental shields to keep any prying minds out. She knew the others with her had done the same. Not all of them could telepathically send messages, but they had all learned how to shield their thoughts. She smiled shyly at the fierce warriors looking at them.

Queen Eleynia took one step forward and drew the attention to herself. She smiled brightly, but looked a little nervous.

Goddess, she's good! Thought Arichel to herself, marveling at her friend. *She is perfect in this role.*

Queen Eleynia and King Daviraf Dafang, the king and queen of Lumos, would lead the group today. They were both excellent at meeting and interacting with new people. Gracious and quick on their feet. Arichel would be able to sit back and observe more if she wasn't the apparent lead of their party.

We got this, Eleynia sent the thought to Arichel, almost as if she could hear her friend's praise.

Daviraf slipped his hand under his wife's arm, and tipped his face slightly deferentially toward the scowling men. However, his eyes never looked down and steadily held their stares. "I wonder if we might be taken to meet your Royal Court?"

The guards, those twelve, thickset, scowling men exchanged glances and then one stepped forward. Speaking to Daviraf and Eleynia he nodded and said, "You will come with me."

"Splendid, Old Chap, so long as you understand that we wish to extend a formal visit to your king and queen."

The man who had spoken never altered his tone or his pace as he walked away, but there was muttering amongst the others. "formal" was all that Arichel could make out. But she saw that their stances relaxed just a touch and grips on spears were a little looser.

Daviraf met her eye and said, "Shall we?"

Arichel nodded almost imperceptibly and fell in step behind Daviraf and Eleynia. Their party spread out three by three alongside her and behind them. The guards gave them space but walked on both sides of their group. They looked like an escort, but the vibe was still guards.

The birds never stopped yammering and the insect buzz began to make Arichel's headache throb just a little more. They followed the path at an easy pace and soon walked through stone arches and what must be the outer gardens of a royal compound. Not long after, they passed through two sets of walls with more of the heavyset, scowling guards. No one seemed surprised to see them now. Whatever their communication was, clearly the twelve guards who met them had somehow sent word ahead.

There was a little fluster of activity just after they entered the immense stone building, with the wide halls. The castle's servants had tried to separate the men and women. Almost immediately an older woman appeared, who glanced at the situation and quickly grasped the problem.

"Ack, me wouldn't separate my people either," she smiled at them. "Our bathing rooms are for just men or women, not commingled ya see. But give me a moment and I'll fix ya up." Her accent was a little different than theirs but the intent was clear.

"Thank you," said Eleynia simply.

The woman bustled off and came back within moments. She shooed off all but four of the guards, who retreated from her almost sheepishly. "This is not me normal hospitality, mind. But I understand wantin' ta stay together on ya first visit."

She led them to a room plainer than the halls, and probably not meant for guests. It was one large room and one washroom off to the side so they could all freshen up. The ladies dutifully washed their faces and their hands. King Tinkerton had quite a sneezing fit after sniffing some sort of potpourri by the one window. The guards had waited respectfully outside the door in the hall. But at Tinkerton's boisterous sneezing, one poked his head in. Seeing him sneezing loudly while still holding the potpourri the guard snickered. He pulled back out to the hallway but reappeared a moment later. With a grin he mimed sneezing then taking a big breath at the fruit he was holding in his hand, and then an exaggerated smile of relief. He held the fruit out to Tinkerton.

Through his sneezes, Tinkerton reached out blindly for the halved fruit and brought it to his face. Immediately, his nose felt worse like a thousand lightning bugs crawling up and blinking their tiny butts through his nasal passages. He swore vehemently and scrubbed at his nose violently. Tinkerton froze. The lightning bug feeling was dissipating and he wasn't sneezing.

Tinkerton looked at the fruit and then back to the guard who was grinning wide. "What the-?"

"Ya, feels weird it does, but it works."

"Thank you!" Tinkerton felt immense relief from no longer bouncing his brain about as he had been while sneezing so violently and continuously.

The guard nodded and stepped back into the hall.

Tinkerton took a moment to wipe his face and to reset his hair with Kri's help.

"Ready?" asked Arichel.

Seeing everyone nod, Daviraf opened the door to move back into the hall.

The four guards were waiting in an escort stance. Tinkerton and one of the guards shared a grin and nod. Arichel was sure that Tinkerton really was being genuinely friendly to the one that helped him, but she was also sure that he would nurture the friendship to see if it could benefit their agenda. She would do the same when she connected with someone.

They walked calmly down the hall, and then to another, and then to a very, very long hall. Once they had reached the third hall they were too far inside the castle to have any windows, but this hall seemed to go on for quite a long while. Too long.

"Very droll, my new friends," began King Daviraf, "but you could perhaps tell me how many more miles of spiraling we must walk before we reach the throne room? I fear the fair ladies, truthfully myself as well, will soon have sore feet if we must continue walking in circles."

Kri gave a start and looked around wide eyed. *I'll be damned.* She said mentally.

Yeah, I missed it, too. Now, I can feel it.

We need to step up our game.

Yeah.

"We are almost there," a stoic guard replied.

The friendly guard shared a quick grin with Tinkerton.

"Well done," Tinkerton said, "I almost didn't realize that there was a spiral. Well done. The slope down is very slight."

Soon enough the party reached the receiving room. Heavy chandeliers hung from the ceiling, the walls were charcoal gray and the rugs were heavy burgundy on black stone. Without the many wall sconces it would have been dark and severe, but the lighting eliminated most shadows, and there was nothing foreboding. Brassy tones welcomed the visitors in. A heavy silence fell and they knew it was expected that they would bow. Arichel and her friends would not bow or subjugate themselves.

Eventually, a regal man stood stiffly to welcome them. As soon as he stood, a young woman stepped forward and in a loud clear voice she spoke, "Here stands The Son of the Heavens, The Caller of the Winds, The Tamer of the Flames, His Most Excellency King Kokaris Fireris." She stepped back and then continued, "Beside his Most Excellency is his beloved wife, The Daughter of the Moon, The Puller of the Tides, Her Majesty Queen Cagne." The queen inclined her head slightly to the guests following her introduction.

In response, King Daviraf stepped forward, inclining his head slightly and introduced his party, "Thank you, King Kocaris and Queen Cagne. Please allow me to introduce my friends and I." Daviraf was often humorous and a bit of a scoundrel, but he could be as formal as anyone. "Beside me here, is my lovely wife, Queen Elenia. Behind her is Ambassador Lath. Next in our group is King Bryongan Le Bryon and Lady Kribell. Following are King and Queen Tinkerton, Queen Arichel, and Captain Adovey." Daviraf was clearly underwhelming their hosts until they had a better feel for the place and the people.

King Fireris motioned with his hand and a curt nod, his purplish black hair falling into his eyes, then two servers stepped forward and knelt in front of Daviraf and Eleynia.

"Here, it is customary to share bread and wine with guests." The regal man spoke softly. He wasn't warmly welcoming but he wasn't the slightest bit rude. Daviraf had the distinct impression he was feeling them out as much as they were him. "Please, break some bread, season it, and enjoy our hospitality."

As he spoke, he broke off a piece of bread and then sprinkled it with salt. He broke it in half, offering a piece to Daviraf and popping the other into his mouth. He then waited while the second servant poured out two glasses from the same decanter and offered both to Daviraf, who solemnly took one. It wasn't foolproof, but the offer was clearly to show that there was no danger of poison. Lath held in the snort that threatened to escape. They all knew that anyone could build a tolerance to any poison if they were very, very careful. Still, it was *probably* safe.

Antidotes? Lath sent to Arichel.

In my purse. She answered.

Lath started, he hadn't even realized that she had a little clutch bag in her hand.

Don't laugh, I know it's not my norm.

Lath bit his cheek, "*Good.*" *Where had she hidden it?* He wondered.

Chapter 13 - Continue the Games

(This chapter is dedicated to Uncle Jeff - we miss you.) The tension lessened in the royal throne room slightly once they had all shared a little bread and wine in the customary welcome ceremony.

"We greatly appreciate your kind hospitality and introducing us to this new custom. We only recently learned of your existence." King Daviraf spoke calmly with some elaborate pauses and hand flourishes. He would stretch this out for as long as he could, as would they all, so that the other party could work unnoticed for as long as possible. Hide and seek on a whole new level while playing charades as well.

And so each member of the entourage gave thanks for their hospitality and commented on some lovely aspect of the decor or their walk to the castle. In response to each greetings and praise, the "foreign" monarchs had to respond in kind.Then there was a symbolic gift given by Daviraf and Elenia and a round of thanks and explanations started all over again. Next came introductions about their countries,...

Captain and Adovey stepped out first, with long practice of immediately standing back to back in a fighting stance. Quickly following behind them jumped Jarrandon and then an outpouring of soldiers. As soon as they saw it was still clear from the scouting two days before, all the troops were called in and gates opened in an orderly staggered foundation (staggering kept them from accidentally setting up on each other if someone made a mistake).

The heat and humidity slammed down on them and sucked their breath away but Jarrandon had warned them, so no one even paused. Just as they had planned, some units spread left and some right and soon they were all spaced out ready to completely surround this mining camp. The same was happening at each of the other mines that Jarrandon had located. Each country had sent their elite and in the teams that worked best together. The only unknown was whether or not an aerial assault would be quickly spotted.

Checking his watch for the coordinated time, Captain gave the nod to Adovey who telepathically sent it to each of the unit leaders here and to the generals at the other mines. Allowing for the ten second delay in relaying messages, all soldiers swept forward at once.

"Tag, you're it!" breathed Adovey.

They knew the risks, but the generals had all agreed that an aerial assault would be initiated first. If it succeeded it could do reconnaissance and a ton of damage in an extremely short time. As the first rocs and firebirds flew over, shouts were heard and then great gongs sounded. But no shots or any kind of weapon seemed to be fired. On the second pass, the riders noted that there were large bonfires being started. It was unclear whether they would produce regular smoke to conceal the camp details or some sort of poisonous gas would rise up. It was agreed to do only one more pass over and then for the riders to stay wherever they could to avoid the smoke. Luckily for them, there was little to no wind.

Illusionists were the second wave, they moved in following the first flyover. They sent all sorts of monstrous beasts charging through camp, complete with the sounds and vibrations. They also began lining up hundreds of soldiers on one side of the camp to try to draw the majority of the defensive over there. The illusion beasts only made one pass through the camp and then stood pawing and rearing on the edge of the trees. It would not be beneficial for someone to recognize them for illusions or note the lack of footprints and therefore lose the elements of surprise.

As the smoke started to rise, a few of the illusionists began to add to the smoke making it appear far more successful than it actually was. Having used this tactic before on battlefields to confuse an enemy, the riders already had specially tinted goggles to easily see through such illusionary "smoke" on their second and third passes.

As they had hoped, the guards dropped to the barest minimum of numbers on three sides and strengthened their forces where they perceived the greatest threat, the lined up illusion forces. Adovey gave the second signal then, and telepathically learned that the scenes at the other mines were similar.

Captain brought a force of young soldiers barreling down on the closest side. Magicians silenced the few guards who noticed them with invisible gags of air. Only a few guards managed to raise an alarm.

***

"So tell me again how it went down?" asked Adovey as they discussed their political and wartime *games*.

"No, ours was boring and stuffy. You had the excitement," argued Arichel.

"It was all important, but she's right. We want to hear about the fight." Krill had dark circles under her eyes and her shoulders drooped. As soon as everyone had gotten back, she had gone straight to the children and helped as many as she could in as many ways as she could. She had been instrumental at setting up locations of food, first aid, showers and clothes before they rescued the children. But she was also the one who thought to gather stuffed toys, sweets, and books for them as they settled into beds or playrooms and waited for their families.

It turned out that Queen Eleynia, queen of Lumos, was very adept at creating fanciful colored shadows that could dance and come alive. Soon the younger children were roaring with giggles as they watched a purple bunny try to sniff a pink flower while a blue grasshopper kept jumping on his head. Later, she transitioned them to a beautiful, and quiet, cascade of fireworks on their ceiling as they fell asleep. The large dormitories had cute little glowing bunnies continuing to hop around and serve as nightlights. They had no idea if the children would have night terrors but the adults were doing all they could to prevent it.

"Well, for a change it actually seemed to go as planned," laughed Captain.

"Yeah, us too," added Lath. "Yours was more fun though."

We were lucky that they were not ready to counterattack any aerial assault-"

"Well they did have a plan for smoking us out of the sky," interrupted Jarrandon.

"Yes, but luckily there wasn't a breeze," agreed Captain. "Our illusionist added to their smoke, so it wasn't nearly as effective as they thought. The illusionists also bought us a nice buffer of safety by drawing most of their forces to defend against illusionary soldiers." He stopped to laugh then, "You should have seen their faces, Krill, the first ones to swing their swords at the charging illusions."

There was a round of chuckling through the room. "They looked so confused, poor souls, when they went to stab and their swords just passed through like cutting air."

Arichel raised her glass of deep, red wine in salute. "Good. I like when the illusions work. Much better for our casualty loss."

"It didn't last long, but it was enough for us to get to the children, calm them, and gather them together."

"We lucked out on that, too," added Jarrandon. "They didn't have any wards or protections set up so we were able to create gates right there and transport the children out immediately."

Riv nodded. "We had a plan to cover them and run out of the camps to where we could set up gates, but this was much, much better."

Daviraf spoke up then, "Our final counts then, are around 300 children from each mine. According to the children, no one was left behind, but that's really hard to tell since we don't even know who they all are, yet."

"What we don't know," said Riv in a sad voice, "is whether there are other mines that Jarrandon hadn't located."

"Right."

Silence fell then as they pondered that. If they had missed a mine, security would be far more intense if they had to break in and rescue more.

"What did your game of hide and seek bring?"

Queen Eleynia tssked, "It was so uncomfortable because they seemed so very nice."

"Right?" asked Jarrandon with a bitter laugh. "They are a *very* hospitable people."

"Yes," agreed Daviraf, "they had a lovely welcome ceremony for us, made extravagant welcome speeches,-"

"Even before that they were nice. They broke their customs to let us freshen up together. And even though he was laughing at me, that guard was awfully nice when I was having my little sneezing fit."

"Little sneezing fit?" snorted Riv.

"Whatever. Fuck off," laughed Lath.

"That's all true. And the bread and wine ceremony. You might want to think of doing something like that, here you know,"

"What?" asked Adovey, a little lost.

"No, it's nothing. It's like the Russian tradition on earth," answered Arichel while waving her hand. "It's a traditional breaking-bread and sipping-wine ceremony. It shows both sides that you don't intend to poison each other-

"A valid concern for them," added Jarrandon.

"True. Anyway, it shows that there is no poison and it allows the hungry guest to have a little snack."

"By the way," snickered Lath, "since when do you carry a purse?" he asked Arichel.

"Only when I absolutely have to," she answered. "It seemed like a good idea to carry some antidotes with me, some basic supplies."

"Weapons?" asked Captain.

"What do you think?"

"Good girl."

Chapter 14 - Now What?!

Evenings are for forgetting but mornings are for reminiscing and regretting.

"Now what? We seem to have two issues."

Lath groaned and covered his eyes. "Can't we just recover? I mean we brought back the kids with no casualties, only bumps and bruises."

"Even the kids are pretty healthy, and damn, they're tough and handling this like champs. Can't we rest for, I don't know, a day maybe?"

There were some chuckles around the room, but no one really laughed. Every person in the room-Arichel, Adovey, Lath, Riv, Kri, Jarrandon, and Captain were all feeling the same.

They were exhausted.

They were also a little satisfied and a little hung over from the battle, the stress, and the after-alcohol.

"Wouldn't that be nice," agreed Riv with a groan.

"Nice maybe," said Captain, "but I think this goes with exactly what we were doing yesterday. I invited our other key players over to discuss it."

Raising an eyebrow, Arichel said, "You did?"

"Uhhuh, House didn't seem to mind." The barest flicker of lights answered.

"Well then, I guess it's settled." Arichel was a little grumpy, overtired mostly, but she was trying to be reasonable. It was just coming out of her mouth in a snarky tone. She stood up and stalked over to the buffet table against the wall.

"If you can't beat 'em, join 'em?" asked Adovey.

"Yeah." Arichel poured herself a glass of blush wine. Variety was good every once in a while. Maybe it would lighten her mood. "Who else wants something?"

Jarrandon came over and between them they served a drink to everyone. Sitting back down, Arichel cracked her neck side to side. Adovey reached over and started massaging it with one hand. She winced in discomfort, but moved her hair out of the way to ease a path for his hand.

Captain threw his head back against the sofa and catnapped. Kri was filing her nails. Riv shook her head at Kri and then stared at her wine, dark red, as if the answers were there.

Soon enough there was a gust of wind from the front door and then in came

Daviraf and Elainia followed by MacKerrit and the lovely Queen Tinkerton.

"My husband will be here shortly," she said with a soft smile. "He lost track of time reading to a group of children. They were quite enthralled, so he wouldn't stop until he got to a chapter break."

"That's awesome," laughed Arichel, genuinely happy.

"Well at least we know who is in charge in that kingdom," laughed Jarrandon.

"He did say, not to wait for him," she continued. "He'll be along shortly."

"Right then." Captain looked around, "Anyone else coming?"

MacKerrit looked around while pouring himself a drink, "I say we start, and as others come in we can catch them up."

"Good enough," said Adovey.

"Right, so as you know, the military action went smoothly yesterday. There were minimal injuries, and as far as we know we collected all the children," began Captain.

Jarrandon jumped in, "Yup, and as far as my other..."

"Spies?" suggested Riv.

"Well, we try not to use that term, but yes. As far as my other intelligence agents can tell, we didn't miss any camps. I think we have all the children."

"It's the spy stuff that seems a bit more complicated in this one. That and damn politics. Give me a battle anyday, over that crap." growled Captain Lath chuckled, "And that is why you're the the one in charge of the military and I'm the ambassador."

"I guess so," grunted Captain. "What else did your spies gather?"

Jarrandon grinned, "It seems that there was quite a commotion in the capital. Some of it started while you all were still there, hence the bells you heard ringing."

"Yeah, it sounded like either a wedding or funeral. There were bells tolling everywhere," agreed Adovey.

"Hush, can ye just let the wee man talk," chimed in MacKerrit.

"Wee man?!"

"Hush," agreed Kri.

"Wee indeed," grumbled Adovey, "He's taller than me.".

Jarrandon chuckled and then continued, "Yeah, so there was a slight commotion. After your stately partly made their grand exit, there were people running all over. We haven't been able to infiltrate the buildings themselves yet, but the chaos was evident outside. Almost immediately after, there were several vehicles of some sort seen rushing out of the royal buildings and then seen arriving not long after at two of the camps. Vehicles were seen at the third too, but I'm not sure where they came from. As far as I can tell, they came from somewhere else."

"Hmm, we need to know where else they came from. That could be important," mused Captain and scrawled something in his pocket notebook.

"Yeah, we're working on that. I'll let you know. We don't really know much about their cities and such. We have figured out some temples, and some sort of colosseum type of place. I think that the colosseum does both fighting and theater *and* music, but we just need more time to see."

"I appreciate that, I'm sure we all do," began Captain and everyone nodded, "but I'm not sure we have time."

"We may not have the time, you're right," agreed Jarrandon, "but that's what I need."

"Aye," agreed Captain. "Ok, well here's what we learned on the streets here," Captain rubbed his cheek with a rough thumb. "The timing almost seems too perfect, and we'll need to confirm of course, but my gut says that this is legit."

"Why?" asked Adovey. He had absolute trust in Captain and wasn't questioning his intelligence, he was just looking for understanding.

Captain nodded, knowing full well that it wasn't his own integrity being questioned. "Well, it was similar conversations in a couple bars and the train station. They weren't verbatim, and one was pretty much all allusion, but it adds up."

"Ok," said Adovey.

"Hold up," said Riv. "Does anything in the past few days seem to relate to the prophecy?"

"Yeah," replied Arichel crankily. "Let's put a pin in that and circle back to it."

"Circle back?" repeated Lath, "really?"

"Shit. sorry, I'm a little overtired, like we all are." Arichel sighed in apology. "You're right, I sounded pompous and ridiculous. Sorry. What I *meant*, was let's handle this first on the face of it, and then circle back to whether these are parts of the prophecy. How we handle it isn't gonna change whether it's prophecy or not, but later, like after a nap, we can consider the wider implications."

"Ok."

House refilled Arichel's wine after hovering two decanters in front of her, one blush and one red. Then, the decanters floated about the room. Bread and butter along with fruit and cold, sliced meats and cheeses appeared too.

Captain continued, "Depending on the source, it seems there is some nobleman or a nobleman's son who has escalated his crazy behaviors. Like before he was wild, and several levels more so than normal, but now there are rumors that he had been locked up at home and has escaped. Some of the rumors suggested he blew up a military camp, but I think that was based on us. The problem is that it seems to be spreading." Captain paused and took a long gulp. "The general conversation seems to be that with hindsight, he was ramping up for a while before anyone really took notice, but now knowing what they know, it seems like other nobles are too."

"Like a gang of degenerates?"

"That's the thing, it doesn't seem to be a group of friends. Acquaintances maybe but not friends."

MacKerrit asked, "Anything in common?"

They all happen to be nobles being talked about here, but maybe it's more widespread than we know. We're still gathering rumors. The working people love to gossip about the nobles after all."

"Hmm," MacKerrit hummed a moment, biting his tongue (quite literally) and then spoke softly. "Earth too."

Lath's head snapped around.

"It's similar," MacKerrit said as he leaned back and tossed an arm up over the back of the sofa he was sitting on. "I asked if there was a connection 'cause I haven't found it on earth yet. To be sure, the rich tend to be arseholes a lot of the time, just 'cause they can and Daddy's money will buy them out. But slowly the gossipers are noticing that it's not one or two that are getting drunkenly violent, but quite a lot of them. Progressively too. Sure, some of them are yacht buddies, but some really don't spend time together in any meaningful way."

"Any theories?"

"Sure, sure. There's always theories. But nothing substantive. Drugs maybe? Hidden messages when the music is played backwards (that held more weight when the music was on a record, by the way, not streamed), new religion, the IRA or other political group - that one is almost me favorite. We never get credit for the good things, though." He paused to chuckle, then asked, "I assume the theories are similar here?"

"Yeah, minus the IRA, but the concept is similar."

"What kind of violence?" asked Eleynia.

"You'll like this: total dismemberment and blood draining." Captain waited for the gasps, "At first the kids, I guess they're not kids, but whatever. Anyway, at first I guess they thought it was someone pretending to be a vampire or some religious cult with a blood obsession. But now they just think it's a lunatic - begging your pardon. No slur intended. Now they just think it's violent craziness."

"No worries, the moon does cause some to be...well, be crazy. She is powerful," Daviraf said. "But they no longer think it's kids playing at vampirism?"

"Nah, it was never about fangs or seemingly to collect the blood, but just rabid violence. Now it's turning from gossip towards fear."

"We need to head that off," said Arichel.

"No doubt," agreed Krill.

"Agreed," MacKerrit nodded. "Ideas?"

They sat silently eating their sandwiches or the fruit for a moment considering.

"This isn't just a distraction, is it?" asked Jarrandon musing.

"From what?" asked Captain.

"I dunno, another kidnapping or something?"

"Fair. We should consider that. But I don't think so."

"Ok."

"That begs the question though," suggested Riv, "Is it a directed thing or an illness?"

"That does alter our strategies."

"The fact that it is both here and earth makes me hope it's directed," said Adovey. Then responding to Arichel's lifted eyebrow, "If it's a disease, or another plague that is spreading it will take an awful lot to figure it out, create a cure, and dispense the cure. If it's people, we just have to find them and kill them."

"True."

"Direct would be better."

"Regardless, we need more information. MacKerrit, what do you need to research this?"

"Some more bodies, preferably discreet and young to blend in."

"Right." Jarrandon nodded, "I'll send some to you. I have an idea of a pair of twins that could "move" to the region you suggest. Can you set up a flat for them?"

"Aye, an extra room for friends, too?"

"Wouldn't hurt."

"Right then, and here?"

"We make sure we're seen, *unafraid*, walking about."

Arichel spoke up, "It's all well and good to solve the mystery, but we also need to calm the people. We just rescued our children, now this? No, we need to reassure the people just as much as anything else."

"You're right," Kri agreed, "we need to solve this and lead by example."

The group nodded.

"Good!" she smiled brightly, "Shopping trip!"

"What?" Lath snorted.

"Shopping trip, dear," Kri smiled sweetly. "We need to stroll the streets and window shop, chatting on the corners with people."

Jarrandon nodded, "Uhhuh, it sets the mood. Plus with chatting you can talk about how well the children are doing and see what you hear. Nice."

Kri nodded her head and grinned, "Exactly."

The days flew by with their different tasks. Arichel balanced her time between being seen out and about in their city and devouring the books that House found for her on this third parallel world, Losunkian.

Now that she knew what she was listening for, Arichel began to hear bits and snatches about mischief and mayhem being caused by young men.

"What we need-" the young woman had waited patiently for Arichel's attention, much to the chagrin of the young man with her. "What we need is a festival or something. A carnival, something to lift everyone's spirits and get back to how we used to feel."

"See, Cherise, I told you not to bother her." The young man tugged at the elbow of the woman.

"No," said Arichel slowly, thinking furiously, "no, don't hurry her off." Arichel smiled at the young man, but then looped her arm through Cherise's other elbow and began walking down the sidewalk. "I think you might be right. Everyone is tense."

"Exactly!" smiled Cherise in relief at being understood. "Like, we all had our worries about getting our work done or talking to our future mother in laws." She blushed and giggled at that. Arichel laughed softly and gave Cherise's arm a gentle squeeze. She was lucky, she actually really liked Adovey's mother and he liked her mother.

"Anyway," Cherise blushed deeper, "We all have our little worries or little spats, but we were pretty happy and relaxed. Now, it's like this great, heavy weight on us all, dragging at us. You rescued those poor children, which helped, but there's still this...I don't know. This anticipation of something more bad to come."

Arichel snapped her fingers. "Yes, that's what I have felt all day. It's an anticipatory dread. You're right, Cherise." Cherise tossed a look over her shoulder at the young man who managed to look proud of her and abashed at the same time.

Arichel bit back a smile and said, "Why don't you come to my house tomorrow morning, both of you, and help me plan something?"

"Oh no, I couldn't! I-"

"And why not?"

"I,I," poor Cherise was at a loss for words. "But I, I have no idea how to plan something like that."

"I'm not sure I do either," laughed Arichel. "That's why we'll figure it out together! Stop by midmorning, alright? Will midmorning work?"

"I, I, um..." Cherise took a deep breath and gave a smile. "Uh, yes.

Midmorning, I'll be there, but I'm not sure he'll want to tag along."

"Fair enough." Arichel smiled in understanding. She turned and spoke to the young man, "But if you do come, I'm sure you can find a man to hang out with at the house, and not be stuck with us ladies planning a party. Unless you want to." His face turned bright red as he stammered his thanks.

Arichel smiled warmly at both of them, then squeezed Cherise' arm again. "I need to go in here, but I'll see you tomorrow, ok?" Cherise looked up and saw that they were outside the university library's side entrance.

"Of, of course, m'lady. Tomorrow then. Midmorning." She didn't know whether to bow, or curtsy, or wave. Arichel saved her by nodding and waving, then whirling about to open the heavy oak door on its silent hinges. After it closed with a solid thud, Cherise noted that there was no doorknob or handle in sight.

Riv grinned, "A carnival or a festival will be perfect! Out in the streets so everyone, regardless of class or social status can attend. Maybe we can get all the nymphs and mystical creatures to come, too!"

"Exactly!" Arichel's eyes sparkled, "We'll send out a global invitation to all our kingdoms, so it will have to be a couple weeks out. But that will just help to build the anticipation."

"And give us time to plan," added Riv.

"Well, yes," agreed Arichel. "She's a little nervous, so I think you should come in a few minutes after she gets here so she isn't overwhelmed with us both at first. Or, you greet her, and settle her, and then I come join you, but not both of us at once."

"Cherise, you said?"

"Uhhuh."

"Ok, either one."

Chapter 15 - Festivus Planning

"Cherise, you said?"

"Uhhuh."

"Ok."

There was a knock at the door and Arichel and Kri held each other's glance a moment. So Arichel turned towards the kitchen, floating towards scents of vanilla and coffee and Kri moved to the door.

Kri's naturally exuberant friendliness shone through as she swung open the door. A moment before, through the frosted glass, she could see Cherise looking back down the walkway as if unsure she should actually be here.

"Come in! Hi! You must be Cherise!" Without letting the poor girl falter, Kri opened the thick door wide and clasped Cherise's hands and pulled her in. Kri grinned and said with a rueful laugh, "Overwhelming isn't it? Coming *here*, to *this* house, not really sure what to do. And then to make it worse some stranger greets you at the door, a little loud and excitable?"

Cherise wasn't sure what to say or do, neither *yes* nor *no* seemed right.

Kri leaned in and whispered conspiratorially, "It's alright, I promise. Just breathe." Kri squeezed her hands gently and pulled her further in. "Here, I'll take your coat and hang it here for you, then we'll go into the library and wait for Arichel, she'll be in shortly with some snacks. We love snacks here."

Cherise was beginning to breathe easier, and handed her coat to Kri, who hung it on a wooden hook, shaped with the other hooks to look like a flower vine, by the door. Her racing heart slowed as they moved to the library, although she sat stiffly on the very edge of the couch.

"Relax, we really don't bite," laughed Kri. "Arichel told me of your idea and I loved it! So, I demanded to be part of the planning. I love a good party!"

At that moment Arichel came in carrying a tray of various cookies and small plates, behind her came a servant carrying drinks and cups.

"Oh good, you're here, Cherise! I see you have met Kri, she's adorable and loves parties!" Arichel laughed at Kri's face when she described her as adorable.

"Just bite me," snorted Kri.

Seeing them acting just like sisters, Cherise started to relax a little more.

"Here," said Arichel, handing Cherise a plate with three different cookies. Then as she began loading a plate for herself, she explained, "The chocolate chip are my favorite, but these here are a little spicy and sweet, and these are made mostly with pumpkin so we can pretend we're being a little healthy." Arichel laughed merrily as she then poured them each a drink. "Tea? Coffee? Milk?"

"Really, Arichel just invited you here so we had an excuse to eat cookies while gossiping and planning a party." Giggled Kri to Cherise as if she were, very obviously, delivering a secret.

It was Arichel's turn to snort a laugh, "Hardly, we would eat the cookies no matter what we were doing. But who doesn't like to plan a good party?"

Several dozen cookies, countless mugs of tea and coffee, and a few interruptions later led Kri, Arichel, Cherise, and Riv (who had joined them midway through) to an easy plan for several simultaneous festivals set up through the city. They were planned so that participants could easily walk from one festival theme to another. Each festival would have its own theme with plenty of food, drink, and music spread amongst them all. They debated for a long time whether to include masks and costumes. It could add a new highlight to the level of fun, however, some people might find it difficult to create a fabulous costume together and no one should feel left out.

"Until tomorrow then," said Cherise as she wrapped herself into her coat.

"Absolutely," answered Arichel, giving Cherise a quick hug.

"Explain to me how a party makes sense?" grumped Adovey as he slumped in a chair at the table, cold beer in front of him.

"Because, Grumpy," explained Arichel with a smile, "We accomplish two things. One, people can go out and have fun, and celebrate the good things of life like this city used to focus on. Annnnd two, it gives a chance to spread out among the people and hear what they are gossiping about, who they are gossiping about, and maybe even seeing this erratic behavior that we keep hearing hints of."

"It's not a bad plan, you know," conceded Lath. "It is the perfect time and space to gather information. Happy people (or really angry people) tend to talk more than worried people. People at a party tend to be happy and talkative. Adding in music, food, and alcohol should loosen even more tongues. It has the potential to be very informative."

"Hmmph."

"You don't have to like it, but you do have to be there looking like you're having fun. Besides, it's live music and booze, how bad can it be."

"Really, really bad," answered Adovey. He understood but he didn't have to like it.

"You get to dress up all pretty..." suggested Lath.

"Pretty?! Well, I do dress up good."

"Maybe I can make it worth your while?" Arichel arched an eyebrow at him.

"Oh yeah?" said a suddenly interested Adovey.

"That-a girl, right to his heart," laughed Lath.

"We'll see," laughed Arichel.

"Do I get to choose how...?" Adovey asked suggestively.

"We'll see," laughed Arichel again.

"Hmmm," Adovey waggled his eyebrows and then got serious. "Ok, what do we need?"

"So with Cherise, we came up with a plan for the entertainment portion-" explained Kri.

"Who's Cherise?" asked Lath.

"A new BFF of Arichel's," giggled Kri.

"Say what?"

Arichel laughed softly, "She's a sweet woman I met while out on the streets the other day. We briefly spoke when I overheard her talking about this feeling of dread hanging over the city. One thing led to another and she helped us plan this whole festival."

"She was a bit nervous, but warmed up," added Riv dryly.

"She was scared out of her mind, you mean," laughed Kri.

"But cookies and coffee put us all at ease."

"They do help," chuckled Lath. "But you wanted us. If you and this Cherise planned it all, what do you need us for?"

"We didn't plan the darker side of it with her," answered Riv.

"We need the security plans in case one of these young men starts acting dangerous or something else. We also need to decide how we gather the most information possible, while seeming to enjoy the party."

"Is this just for our city?" asked Captain, "Or are we inviting the other courts and people?"

"We want it to be the *event of the season*," answered Kri. "Yes, we figure we want to have all the possible people here."

"Right, so this is the preplanning, planning," said Lath.

"Right."

"Ok, so how many venues, how do we spread, and what do we particularly want to hear, is what we need to figure now. Then, invite the other courts to discuss the same things with us," suggested Lath.

"Yup, that pretty much sums it up."

"Ok," Adovey poured wine for everyone else and more beer for himself.

"Is it four themes?" clarified Captain.

"Uhhuh, one for each season."

"Ok, so there are four places to divide us. It would be odd for you two to separate," Captain nodded at Arichel and Adovey. "So maybe we very carefully have you float amongst all the events. That won't raise suspicions and maybe make it less obvious that we're spread out. Especially as the others spread out, too. I don't think it should be a full court at each location, but mixed."

"Agreed," said Lath. "Both from what guests will notice, but also because we all have our inherent habits, suspicions, etc, so a greater variety of audience of us at each location is better."

"Ok, so Riv, Kri, Lath, and I all choose one location to be at. Any preferences?" asked Captain.

"I prefer winter generally, so I'll take that festival," said Riv.

"I don't have a preference."

"Me either."

"Well I like summer," said Kri, "you two can fight over fall and spring."

The men looked at each other and shrugged.

"Yup."

"Sounds good."

"Ok, let's invite the others to dinner tonight or tomorrow and hash out what we think we need to look for. And obviously whatever else strikes us we'll report back, too."

"Yup. Dinner tonight would be nice, but I suppose they do have lives after all," sighed Adovey.

"You might just have to wait a little," laughed Arichel.

"I'm not exactly a patient person."

"Oh, we know!"

"You should distract me."

"Oh yeah?" Arichel asked with raised eyebrows and trying to hold back a smile.

Adovey bit his bottom lip, "Uhhuh."

"I need to distract you, huh?"

"Definitely," he smacked her ass lightly as she went up the stairs in front of him. "Now that," he said appreciatively "is distracting."

"Then I guess I don't have to do anything except walk in front of you."

"That would work,...but I have a better idea." As he said that, they were at the door in front of their room. House obligingly unlatched it as Adovey picked Arichel up. She wrapped her legs around his waist, letting the heat from her core lay right against him. Her arms wrapped around his neck and his mouth captured hers. He used her body to push open the door and stumbled in as they kissed, deeply and full of emotion. The door softly closed behind them.

He dropped her on the bed and then crawled over her, pinning her down and capturing her mouth again. The kiss became fierce as they each nipped at lips, sucked at tongues, and swept tongues over teeth.

They drew back for a moment to breathe while laughing softly. "Or, we could do this."

"Uhhuh."

His hands grabbed at her skirt and tugged it down and off, then her leggings which tangled at her feet. Arichel sat up to wiggle her ankles through and kicked off the leggings. Then she leaned over, unbuttoning his pants. She slid his pants and boxers down and over his knees. Teasing his cock with fingers just barely grazing it. She leaned down and breathed hot breath onto him. He growled softly and used his feet to shove off his pants the rest of the way. She laughed.

"Oh yeah?" Adovey reached and grabbed a fistful of her hair, not hurting, but forcefully pulling her down. She danced her tongue at the very tip, then a harder lick just under the foreskin crown. He gasped and sucked his bottom lip between his teeth. She tapped his hand to have him loosen his grip so she could move. He immediately let go. She pressed her tongue hard against his hard cock and traced the vein all the way to the base and back up again. Then again using her lips to suck at it, down and back, but over the top this time. Her lips encircled the head so she could flick her tongue around it,

Old hand at this, she knew how hard to pull and tease his balls, she knew where he liked the pressure of her tongue. The question was how fast to adjust her tempo, and whether he wanted deep or shallow. She paid attention to his sounds, his quickened breathing, whether his stomach muscles twitched and whether his hands grasped at the sheet.

Unwilling to wait longer, he growled and pushed her away and onto her back. She scooted up the bed and he moved down between her legs. He dragged her thong off and then swept his tongue from her ass to her clit. Then he laid down, used his thumbs to spread her lips wide and seriously got to work. As good as she was with giving him head, he was like a magic snake with his tongue.

Adovey started with slow, lazy swirls, knowing that she needed a moment to slow her thoughts and clear her mind. Then, he began to increase the pressure and flick her clit. Almost immediately then, he began to focus entirely on her clit, teasing her nerves to his will. His hands moved to the inside of her thighs and softly but firmly rubbed and squeezed. The speed of his tongue increased as one hand moved up to her lower stomach and pulled against the skin ever so little, adding just a little stretch to the clit, exposing it ever so much more. At the same time he slid a finger into her wetness and moved it in a curling "come here" motion. Feeling her muscles tighten and begin to quiver, he swiped a thumb across her ass. Her stomach clenched, as he continued to flick his tongue. She rode the climax through and then she pushed herself back a little. Adovey sat back then and grabbed the blanket to wipe his face. "Did you enjoy that?" he asked with a smirk.

"Obviously," she chuckled. Arichel twisted about so she could reach her hand to wrap around his cock where he sat. "Now what?"

"Roll over."

Arichel rolled over on her belly, her left hand up by her face. She moved her right arm under and between her legs, as Adovey straddled over her. Stretching her arm as far as she could, she could just barely reach his cock, which hardened again at her touch and more so as he leaned forward feeling her hot, wet, and ready for him.

He nudged his cock against her, and she pressed with her middle fingers to guide him in and hold him there. He began to stroke in and out, slowly savoring the feeling. She kept her fingers tight against him so he wouldn't slide out all the way.

Just then, there was a gentle brush at her mind, the equivalent of a telepathic, soft knock. Adovey must have felt her tense up. "Fuck, they're here, aren't they?" He stroked faster.

Arichel opened her mind and Jarrandon's voice spoke softly, "Sorry to interrupt, Love, but we have company. Dress up a little when you come down, I said you were in a meeting."

She sent a wicked smile and a naughty picture back.

Jarrandon groaned, "You're wicked!"

Arichel felt Jarrandon pull back. She turned her head and spoke out loud, "Apparently we have company, but he bought us a little time saying we were in a meeting. He said to dress up a little when we come down, so it must not be *our* people."

"I love that man!" chuckled Adovey. Then he leaned forward and nipped her ear, "Not as much as I love you, though."

Adovey put his weight on his elbow and his hand around her throat. He began thrusting again, more powerfully this time. She moved her hips to meet him, arching her back, and pressing with her fingers against his cock. Faster and harder they drove against each other. He pulled back and hesitated and then dove deep and deeper still. She could feel him pumping, and then slowly softening. They lay together like that for a moment, panting and just mellowly resting into each other.

"I suppose," Adovey groaned and rolled off of Arichel, "that we should go down and see who is here."

"Yeah, probably." Arichel stretched her neck and then rolled off the bed. She hurried into their bathroom to clean up, and they quickly dressed. Stepping into the hallway, as she finished twisting a braid and pinning it up, they heard raised voices from downstairs.

They paused at the top of the stairs to listen, Arichel sending her awareness down to her friends downstairs. Riv sat examining her nails by the fire, Lath sat on the arm of the chair next to her. Captain swirled a glass of wine as he negligently leaned against the fireplace. MacKerrit and Kri leaned back on the couch. Two men and a woman, stood just inside the living room. The shorter of the two was blustering his point to his very uninterested audience.

Chapter 16 - Festivus

The day dawned clear and bright. Arichel and Jarrandon stepped out for a morning run that just happened to include the four locations of the festival that night.

"I know he's a pompous jerk, but we have to check, right?"

She grunted her agreement. Arichel hated to talk and run. Running was her mental break, when her feet could pound out her frustration or her worries. She could focus on the pain of the next mile, set mini goals of running to just the next street or sprinting over the next rise.

Instead of turning to the woods as she wanted to, Arichel and Jarrandon started jogging down the hill towards the great bridge. The River Gwen split the city in half and "The Bridge" connected it. There was a metal plaque on the bridge with an official name, but no one ever used it; it was just The Bridge.

As their muscles stretched and warmed up they picked up their pace. Birds chattered overhead, and there was just a light breeze to tickle their faces as they ran towards the red orange sun. Truly, Jarrandon could run faster, but ultimately Arichel could run longer. Typically they found a pace that they could both run at for a good hour and both be winded, but not too sore from it.

Today, Arichel's head was all over the place and she had to consciously keep relaxing her shoulders. She kept thinking back to a conversation from three weeks earlier when the three visitors showed up to her house. The visitors were heated, but her court stayed calm until after the three left. Then, two wine glasses from opposite sides of the room were both hurled at the fireplace, and the swearing could have turned the air blue.

Now, instead of clearing her mind and finding calm, her pounding feet hurled the angry words and accusations around in her head. She unclenched her jaw, and loosened her shoulders again, dropping her hands and purposely swinging them to bump her thumbs into her hips. It was an old trick she used and one that Jarrandon instantly recognized- as if the wall of steel clamped down around their telepathic link wasn't enough. He knew she wasn't keeping him out so much as keeping her anxiety, anger, and frustration in. So he just ran beside her, waiting for her to leash her emotions or to decide to talk.

The past week had been full of activity here, but Arichel and Adovey had been in the mortal realm of earth, balancing her time between parallel worlds. The governments there had apparently decided that they had succeeded in "flattening the curve" and life was returning to normal without an obnoxious mystery virus impacting them anymore. A mystery virus that had no definitive source and seemed to have just disappeared...
The only notable thing, other than life returning to normal, was the appearance of Hilliel. About every eighty years or so he would appear. He would be around for a while and then disappear. The mortals believed that he was from an odd family that named one son from each generation with the old family name of Hilliel. He let them believe this. The family estate was there, the estate paid all its bills and kept a minimal staff in expectation of the family's imminent return.

But Arichel didn't buy it. Nor did she play games, so one day she just asked him. Hilliel laughed long and loud and gave her a boisterous hug lifting her nearly two feet off the ground.

"You lass, are the very first in more than a thousand years to ask me this. I'm going to like you!" When she was set down and could breathe again, they chatted for hours over wine.

"I'm assigned to earth, but I'm not very good at following the rules. Hence the fact that I just got out of prison."

Assigned to earth. "I see." But she didn't see, not really.

"No you don't, but you will."

"Ok."

He filled their glasses again and leaned back. "I'm an angel, but I'm not very angelic. Michael has almost given up on me, until we agreed to just let me do my own thing to right the wrongs, and not expect him to step in and save my ass from the consequences of my actions."

"Uhhuh." It wasn't any clearer yet.

"You see, angels are supposed to be all sweet and non judgemental while being righteous and saving those in distress who are good of heart, and all that bullshit." Arichel nodded and he continued, "But there's no way to actually do that without being judgmental, see?"

"I follow you."

"Right. So if we can judge some things, then we can judge it all. I tend to be the judge, jury, and executioner. But then the law sometimes gets involved. Prison isn't all that bad though. Especially when I know I sent some asshole to a far worse place. I really don't like the people who beat on those weaker than them."

"But you're immortal, how does prison work? I mean, don't they notice you always look the same age?"

"Well, there's that. Turns out most humans just can't accept what their eyes see and figure there must be some sort of mistake. After like fifty years or so they generally let me out on good behavior assuming that my original sentencing date must be wrong somehow. No one works in a prison that long so no one really recognises me." He chuckled again, "One time the parole board actually said my behavior had been angelic, 'You have no idea' I said."

"Yeah, I bet!" Arichel laughed too. "They never figure it out?"

"Nope, they see what they expect to see. There was one time though that I spent like two hundred years in a cell. Pretty sure they forgot I was there. Eventually there was an earthquake and I escaped through the rubble."

"So now you're just going to hang around until you find someone else who needs punishment?"

"Or, someone who needs rescuing. That's more my style."

"I see."

***

Arichel and Jarrandon ran through the streets as they checked the festival sites for anything odd, or any strange energies. By the time they cut through the park of the second site, Arichel's mind had calmed down and her focus was returning. They had a solid plan for safety and had set plans for eavesdropping and gathering information. They might even be able to enjoy Festivus themselves. Finally, her mind cleared about Hilliel, the rogue angel, as well. Her pace had smoothed out and her energy was vibrant and calm again, not skippy and haphazard as she started out.

"Better now?" Jarrandon asked as they ran.

With her pace staying even, Arichel laughed a little and said, "Yeah. I guess you could say that. I needed this."

"I know. We both needed the exercise, but you needed the mind space, too."

They lapsed back into silence, not needing to talk and each content to push their pace and their minds, but not talk. Sweat began to trickle down her back and collect under her breasts. Jarrandon swiped an arm across his forehead. Sweat therapy was the best therapy.

Dawn had come and gone, but the morning hush still hung in the air as if the day was just holding back and waiting. Their feet hit solidly on the dirt paths and thwacked against the sidewalks, slapping sounds against the quiet. Ragged breath and swinging arms were their other noises. This wasn't the time for stealth and it felt good to just run. Arichel's hair was pulled back in a ponytail and it both swung side to side and streamed out behind her. It would be a mess to brush out, but completely worth it for this hour or so of freedom. This hour of not being queen, or the binder of worlds - not in control of anything except her run. Right now she was just a runner and that was enough. But to sweeten it, she was running beside one of her best friends and they were just enjoying being together. They saw each other at their best and worst, a little workout sweat was nothing.

Finally having visited each festival site, and the bridge, they ended with jogging up the stairs to the city wall. From up there you could see for miles, and it was the ideal place to slow to a walk and stretch out. It had perfect little spots to lean and stretch and hardly anyone came up here. There were sentries posted, of course, but they simply nodded greetings as they recognised the regular runners.

One of Jarrandon's favorite stretch spots was a long view towards the east. The mountains and hills fit together just right so that there was a single valley of sight for hundreds of miles. On a clear day, and when you weren't looking at the rising sun, you could imagine that you could just barely glimpse the ocean. They stopped here, stretching and then just leaning against the wall's rail. Their elbows pressed together as they leaned, looking out.

"We should do some "tours" of the country again," mused Arichel.

"Hmm?"

"I mean, we're making a point to be seen out and about in the city, but we need to be out and about in the country too."

"Hmm."

"But not a stupid political stunt. Something genuine." She paused and chuckled. "Which is why we haven't done it. There is not anything that we genuinely need outside of the city, unless we're visiting other courts."

They both were silent in thought for a minute.

Jarrandon spoke, "Ask Captain if there are some trainings that you can go to."

"What? I don't want to train."

"Why not, you're good enough to train with the legions, the women anyway. Might be some good morale building that way, too. But you could just do some visits to the training facilities.

We really should have you and Adovey to do that anyway. Not that we don't trust Captain, we obviously do, but just, y'know."

"The royal personna checking in, raising spirits, reminding them who they are?"

"Something like that." He laughed low in his throat. "You'd probably have more fun doing a training session though. Less talking involved. And it wouldn't matter if you were better, held your own, or lost your ass. They would respect you either for your ability, your effort, or for the fact that you appreciate them protecting you."

"Hmm. Maybe." She chewed her lip for a moment. "I would rather be on par with them though. Maybe I should have some practice sessions first."

"Pretty sure you can hold your own. But if you're going to do mud wrestling, I get to watch."

"Asshole!" She punched him lightly on the shoulder and they both laughed. "Yeah, I'll talk to Captain, and see what he says about joining some training. Not-" she grinned, "not any wrestling though."

"Awww, you're no fun. I would help you wash off and check you over for bruises," he offered suggestively.

"Oh, I'm sure. But no, I'm set on that, thanks."

Jarrandon and Arichel jogged back to the house at an easy pace, still laughing about not mud wrestling as they came through the door.

"Enjoyed your run?" asked Adovey with a smile.

"Oh yeah. His assholeness here thinks I need to take up mud wrestling. Not you, too! You're both assholes." Arichel punched Adovey in the arm too, as he grinned in appreciation of the image. "Whatever, I'm going to go shower alone, you can both imagine that."

"Alone?"

"Yes, alone!" She laughed as she ran up the stairs.

Riv was standing at the top of the stairs, having been listening. She chuckled low, "You're mean. They'll be hot for you all day."

"Yup!"

***

The gates began to pop in the early afternoon with their friends arriving from other courts. People had been streaming into the city for the past few days, and today the roads into the city were flooded. The stillness had evaporated just as Jarrandon and Arichel had finished their morning run. House was busy materializing clean towels and ironing outfits for the guests as they arrived. Kitchen staff were busy prepping a light meal and drinks for everyone as they gathered at the table, in the gardens, and as they rested in their rooms.

In the later afternoon, they met around the table to chat together and to plan their evening.

"Ok," Lath stated. "We have our home girls managing the Summer and Winter festivals with Jarrandon and I managing Spring and Autumn.

Captain is bouncing around as needed, just like Arichel and Adovey are traveling to all the festivals. I know we all agreed to break up our courts to all the festivals, so you all have a plan to split at each festival, too?" Seeing their nods, "I don't think we really need a list of who is going to be where, do we?"

"Probably not."

"Nah,"

"We're not wearing masks, so it's easy enough to find each other."

"True."

"Yeah,"

"Alright," said Adovey, "and we all meet back here eventually.

"Good enough, let's go get ready. Ladies, we're meeting in my room!" sang out Kri.

"We have time for another drink," sighed Lath.

"Or three," added Adovey drily.

"We will be too, don't worry," laughed Eleynia.

"Most assuredly," agreed Riv.

"That's it! Get your drink on."

"Uhhuh!"

Chairs scraped as the ladies pushed back and hurried up to Kri's room to begin dressing and styling their hair. A breeze had picked up but it seemed like it would be a delightfully warm evening.

"We checked the sites this morning," said Arichel as she threaded blue sapphires into Kri's hair. "There is plenty of open space at each site. Then a pavilion or tent in the middle, a staged off area for the musicians, and another area for food vendors to line up. Each locale either has one central point that you can see everywhere, including in the tent or at most we have to split into two clumps to see everywhere. It shouldn't be too obvious that we're watching everywhere, especially if we keep trading off."

Riv added, "And because each location is small, it should be pretty easy for the rest of us to move about and hear a lot of conversations. It seems like a solid plan." She smiled viciously, "We might even be able to have a little fun."

"Oh no," laughed Kri, "Which young lad's heart are you toying with now?"

"Why would you think there is just one?"

"Fair."

"You go, girl!"

Just then the entire house, maybe the entire mountain shook and rumbled. The mirror tipped and fell to the floor, wine glasses shattered, and the lights flickered, went out and came back on a moment later. The whole house vibrated as if House were being pulled in two directions and refusing to rip. A window pane cracked. The rumbling decreased and stabilized, and bells began to clang in the city.

The women sprang to the window and looked out over the city. Tendrils of smoke lazily climbed to the sky from several directions and more bells began to toll.

Mental conversations began flying through the house with each person vocalizing what they knew. Everyone hurried from where they were, to the upper story of House and out onto the balcony for a better view. Up here they could see completely over the city and beyond the walls.

Messages began popping out of the air and materializing by the score. "Fuck!" said both Captain and Jarrandon at the same time, tossing the messages they had read to the others. They headed to the door and pounded down the stairs.

"On our way to the barracks!" Jarrandon threw the mental shout to Arichel.

"What the actual fuck?!" she asked out loud.

"It's that new parallel world. Losunkion," said Eleynia dully, setting down the message she had read.

"Look," said Riv pointing westward.

"The dragons," breathed Arichel.

They watched as the dragons came closer and then swooped in and roared at the forest.

"Are they on our side?" asked Kri.

"It appears so," stated Riv as she watched a section of trees torn out and then Losunkions suddenly charred as their cover was ripped away.

Arichel and Adovey both spun simultaneously and hurtled to their room. House already had laid out their fighting leathers and a variety of weapons for them to choose from.

"Thank you, House," said Arichel

Plop.

A book appeared on the bed.

"House, there isn't time for reading right now-" started Adovey. But Arichel paused from buckling and belting her vest, understanding that House wasn't just offering a bedtime story.

Battle tactics of the Lonsunks

Losunks, Losunkions, close enough, thought Arichel. She sat on the bed and began paging through.

The house shuddered again and a second later there was a supersonic boom.

"Damn!"

A shadow passed the window and a second later the belly and legs of a dragon swooped past the window.

"We have got to get out there!" shouted Adovey.

"Yeah, give me a minute. This may help."

Adoved leaned down and kissed her. The same deep kiss as he gave her when she was challenged by Bryongen to the duel. A kiss that held everything just in case they wouldn't kiss again.

***

Other stories by Rachel Roy:
Adult:
Throu[1]g[2]h the Gate[3](adult fantasy romance) The Inn-Between at Burkl[4]y[5]n[6] (adult romance) Homesteading trilogy (nonfiction):
How to Be[7]g[8]in Homesteadin[9]g[10]
How to Make Mone[11]y[12] on Your Homestead[13]
Our Homestead Reci[14]p[15]es[16]

---

1. https://www.amazon.com/kindle-vella/story/B09YY549SQ

2. https://www.amazon.com/kindle-vella/story/B09YY549SQ

3. https://www.amazon.com/kindle-vella/story/B09YY549SQ

4. https://www.amazon.com/kindle-vella/story/B0BJB1PJXZ

5. https://www.amazon.com/kindle-vella/story/B0BJB1PJXZ

6. https://www.amazon.com/kindle-vella/story/B0BJB1PJXZ

7. https://books2read.com/u/m2edy1

8. https://books2read.com/u/m2edy1

9. https://books2read.com/u/m2edy1

10. https://books2read.com/u/m2edy1

11. https://www.amazon.com/kindle-vella/story/B09TYJXS1S

12. https://www.amazon.com/kindle-vella/story/B09TYJXS1S

13. https://www.amazon.com/kindle-vella/story/B09TYJXS1S

14. https://www.amazon.com/kindle-vella/story/B0B4R69R29

15. https://www.amazon.com/kindle-vella/story/B0B4R69R29

16. https://www.amazon.com/kindle-vella/story/B0B4R69R29

Children's and Young Adult:
Growin[17]g[18] U[19]p[20] As Fairies[21](children's fantasy)
The Summer House[22](children's fantasy)
The Breakin[23]g[24] of the Universe[25] (YA fantasy)

17. https://books2read.com/u/bW5MJ7

18. https://books2read.com/u/bW5MJ7

19. https://books2read.com/u/bW5MJ7

20. https://books2read.com/u/bW5MJ7

21. https://books2read.com/u/bW5MJ7

22. https://www.amazon.com/The-Summer-House/dp/B09YVLNVHH

23. https://www.amazon.com/kindle-vella/story/B0BQ3XRJXM

24. https://www.amazon.com/kindle-vella/story/B0BQ3XRJXM

25. https://www.amazon.com/kindle-vella/story/B0BQ3XRJXM

THROUGH THE GATE

By Rachel Roy

Prologue

She walked through the gate and up the long drive, tossing the events of the day through her mind. She stopped walking before she realized why. She had just rounded the last bend when she had stopped, and now her eyes darted over the several black suv's and limo in her drive. More than that her attention was on the men in uniform standing around the vehicles. One uniformed man was just stepping out of the house, slamming the door behind himself.

"I see you, Alder." The soft gravelly voice stopped her in her tracks before Joneya slipped back behind the bend, back to safety. *Damn.* That greeting gave so much information at once. Her eyes snapped shut so her brain could process faster, she cart wheeled through time to her childhood and back again. Sir Ned would come out of the shadows and softly say 'I see you' when he had to pull her back to duties. It was their code to know that even while she successfully hid from everyone else, that he, her guardian, could find her and now it was time to return. And now he said those words again. After a decade, she had hoped this time her hiding spot might last.

Rough hands grabbed Joneya. "I got her!" yelled a voice. The hands pulled her arms forward, but she held her feet rooted still.

"Release. Her. Now." That soft gravelly voice could also be hard and cold, seemingly booming loud even though it was a quiet voice. The hands immediately released, and she felt the men step back.

Alder. That simple nickname held so much information too. First, he wasn't using her given name, that was for her safety. It was one of many call signs used for her when her name couldn't be spoken over radio communication, but this one he used to her face when he needed her to know that the formality was much more than politics and royalty. It was about something older and deeper and of The Family. Alder was her druidic sign, but almost no one knew that, true birthdays were kept secret. *The wind might blow as it may, but we must bend before the wind to be strong.*

Joneya opened her eyes, "The wind blows as it may. I see thee, Sir Hand."

His eyes barely lowered in a nod and his smile almost showed before Sir Ned was stone faced again. They stared at each other for a moment. He had more gray and wrinkles and yet seemed hardly changed. She, on the other hand, had grown up from the twenty-something runaway to the thirtysomething woman standing before him. So much like her mother. Their eyes locked for a moment. Then, she glanced to the house, he nodded so she walked in as he followed. So did three other men in uniform.

"I'm sorry, my Lady." Her eyebrows moved at the change of address. Again, four words with so much information. Apparently, the queen was dead, which meant what exactly? The daughter heir had died years ago in a tragic accident, which left whom in the royal line? Oh the feuding would be epic! But clearly the news hadn't hit the AP wire yet, or she would have seen or heard already.

Her eyes flicked over the men, she didn't know the three who had followed them in. "I did not expect this news today." No tears for the woman who had always been a room away. Or more often, an entire neighborhood away. Sir Ned and his wife had cleaned up more of her scraped knees than the woman with the beautiful long hair, pristine gowns, and the diamond crown. She had nothing in common with that woman. Well, very little.

Sir Ned, also known by his title, The Hand of the King. Except truly, his title was, Angbor D'elyar - Fist of the Blood. Most people assumed Blood meant the royal bloodline and so the title had changed in the common tongue. Some remembered that the powerful families of old were not always those of the royal lineage. Though to be fair, often the royal lineage was based upon the ones who held the power. Quite a few believed the power, then and now, was of the old ways. Few claimed to be a druid now, but every child of the "powerful" families played a game when they were young. That game had them guessing the secret code, by looking at symbols and lines. If they decoded the first secrets on paper, they then moved to the second level and tried to read the secrets on the rock. Very few children were ever able to read the secrets, and those who did, kept the secrets safe. Sir Ned played the game with Joneya. The secrets had inevitably led her to this day.

"Sir Ned, my children will be home soon." She stated this not as a question nor as an imperative, but to state the information to formulate a plan forward.

"Yes." Sir Ned nodded. "Would you care for assistance packing a bag for the next day?"

"Only for a day?" She arched an eyebrow slightly.

"You only need to pack for a day, my Lady." *Was there a slight emphasis on pack?* His answer was clarified when Sir Ned continued, "The men will close up the house, and two men will stay here. As to your dog,..."

Joneya did smile internally then, picturing the men as they tried to command the 140 pound Rottweiler to do anything that he didn't want to. Most likely he had allowed them into her room and then had them frozen in place, terrified to move another inch or be eviscerated. "My puppy will come with me."

"Yes. Of course. Could you perhaps convince your, um, puppy to allow the men to breathe again?" She could hear the smile he was holding back.

"I could. But, I may not. They have no business in my room."

"Lady, we were just-" began one of the men in uniform.

"Silence." Joneya and Sir Ned said in unison. She continued on, "I am not happy that you are here, in my home. I understand you are here by orders, not by choice. I, however, am a bitch by choice *and* family curse. I will *not* tolerate certain things and an invasion into my, or my children's space, is one of those things I will not tolerate. In the future, you would all do well to stay out of my personal quarters unless invited. Nor, for the record, do I tolerate lying, thieving, or hypocrisy. If you intend to stay in my employ, or my proximity, I expect respect." Softer she continued, "In return, I will respect you. If you do not follow this simple philosophy, I will make your life a living hell. You should explain this to your friends. And perhaps, your enemies as well."

"Yes Ma'am." The poor man-boy looked like he might swallow his tongue and certainly wished he might be able to escape immediately.

"*My* Lady, the men, your dog. Please." Sir Ned was indeed still a man of few words, as if secrets might spill if he used too many words.

She met his eyes, frowned, and acquiesced. At Joneya's first whistle she knew his ears perked forward. At her second whistle he stood up, the five of them could hear his nails on the floorboards above. At her third whistle, a different note combination, the puppy came tearing down the stairs, bounding across the room, and sat at attention by her hand. She laid her hand upon his head and rubbed behind his ears. "Good boy, Sere*." She raised an eyebrow at the three man-boys, they shuffled their feet and avoided her eyes. Except one, the one she had just chewed out.

He grinned. "Nice, my Lady. Very nice." She smiled then; he had potential.

*Sere - peace.

Chapter 1

The two children boarded the plane beside her. The dog, Sere, followed so closely that he kept stepping on their heels despite their scolding. The children were a little nervous, quite excited, and a bit confused. Joneya was not particularly nervous (not at all for the plane ride), and was considering a tattoo of a strong, bending tree. *We must bow before the wind if we wish to weather the storm.* This would be the storm of the century.

They boarded the private jet, led and followed by uniformed men. "Mom," the seventeen year old boy with piercing blue eyes asked, "how long is this flight?"

"I'm not sure exactly." She replied. "We'll have plenty of time to get settled, eat supper, watch a movie or read, and then go to sleep. Sleeping may be hard, but tomorrow is going to be very busy and it will be tomorrow when we land."

"Wait!" said the blond haired girl with the long ponytail. "We're eating supper on the plane?"

"Yes." Smiled the woman. "Or else we'll be really hungry. We can't land on the ocean, get out and eat." She could see Sir Ned biting his cheek to keep from laughing. The blond haired girl rolled her eyes. "Obvs. What are we eating?"

"I don't know. But I'm sure they have planned ahead to accommodate what we like." Joneya knew it was a little overwhelming to be basically ripped out your home after school. It would only get worse. She could explain everything in detail or she could be nonchalant about some of it. There were no parenting handbooks that covered this and her own mother hadn't prepared her at all.

"But they're definitely meeting us here?" asked Elfrya's ponytail swung as she peered around.

Sir Ned cut in, "I assure you child, we will not leave without the rest of your family." And just like that, the concerns that Joneya had about her blended family being pushed apart, were evaporated like a popping soap bubble.

Just then, a loud, familiar 12 year old's voice could be heard, "This is dope. How long is this tunnel? In the movies they're really short. Is this what you go on all the time, Arigail?"

"I'd say they're here," said Larseth dryly.

As Larseth spoke, Joneya's husband, Abaris stepped onto the plane followed by his son and daughter. His eyes immediately found hers, and she smiled in welcome. "You ok?"

"Yeah." There really weren't words to explain all the emotions raging through her. But she pushed them all aside to rage like winds in a storm, set her roots deep, and went with the flow. "I'd like you to meet Sir Ned. The most honorable man I know."

As soon as Abaris saw she was ok, the tension went out of his shoulders. The men shook hands, judging each other, and a little surprised at each other's strength of character. Ever the impatient one, Arigail grabbed Ravous' hand and darted over to Elfrya. The four kids wandered forward in the plane, which was nothing like any of them had been on.

Ravenous' voice floated back, "It's like Air Force One, this plane."

"We'll be taking off directly, m'lady." said Sir Ned. "Make yourselves comfortable."

Table of Contents

Dedication

Parallel Worlds

Chapter 1 - The Duel

Chapter 2 - The Message

Chapter 3 - The Meeting

Chapter 4 - Humanity and Houses

Chapter 5 -The Plague

Chapter 6 - A Summons

Chapter 7 - Envoys

Chapter 8 - The Library Chapter 9 - Waiting

Chapter 10 - A little Pet

Chapter 11 - Reunited

Chapter 12 - Hide and Seek

Chapter 13 - Continue the Games Chapter 14 - Now What?!

Chapter 15 - Festivus Planning

Chapter 16 - Festivus

Through the Gate

Don't miss out!

Visit the website below and you can sign up to receive emails whenever Rachel Roy publishes a new book. There's no charge and no obligation.

https://books2read.com/r/B-A-EEVR-EZSHC

BOOKS 2 READ

Connecting independent readers to independent writers.

About the Author

Rachel Roy lives in the Northeast Kingdom of Vermont with her husband and children. She has been writing for as long as she has known that people could create books. In 2021, her first children's story, Growing Up As Fairies, first appeared on Kindle Vella in serial format. After edits and illustrations she published it in print in December 2022. In the meantime she added six other series to Kindle Vella including another children's story, two non-fiction homesteading resources, and several fantasy and fantasy romances. Rachel also teaches middle school Humanities as she continues to write.

Read more at https://www.authorrachelroy.com.